Robert B. Parker

CEREMONY
A Spenser Novel

G.K.HALL &CO.
Boston, Massachusetts
1985

Published in Large Print by arrangement with
Delacorte Press/Seymour Lawrence.

G. K. Hall Large Print Book Series.

Set in 16 pt Plantin.

ISBN 0–8161–3833–8

To Joan, for whom the sun does in fact rise and set— or would if she told it to.

The blood-dimmed tide is loosed, and
    everywhere
The ceremony of innocence is drowned. . . .

from 'The Second Coming,'
by William Butler Yeats

CHAPTER ONE

'She's a goddamned whore,' Harry Kyle said. 'And I don't want her in this house again.'

'For God's sake, Harry, you're talking about your own daughter,' his wife said.

'She's a goddamned whore,' Harry said.

'You don't know that, Mr. Kyle,' Susan said.

'The hell I don't. I saw her in there hanging all over some guy older than me. I saw what she was doing and she can keep right on doing it, because she ain't coming back here.'

'That doesn't make her a whore, Mr. Kyle.'

'Don't tell me what it makes and doesn't make, lady. I don't need some goddamned goody two-shoes coming around and giving me a lot of that bleeding-heart mumbo jumbo they teach nowadays.'

'Harry,' I said.

Susan looked at me. The look said *shut up*. A lot of people looked at me like that, but to Susan I paid attention. We were standing in the perfect living room of a perfect house in a perfect development in Smithfield. The

1

upholstery was all in powder blue and the rug and walls and drapes all coordinated with it. The furniture was massive Mediterranean oak, probably—dark stained. You could tell they'd bought it all at once. It was a set, a living room set. I was willing to bet my new blackjack that there was a dining room set in the dining room and at least four bedroom sets upstairs. The cellar probably had a cellar set, all coordinated with the furnace.

Kyle was tall and fat and with an unhealthy flush to his face and fleshy neck that spilled over his shirt collar. He'd made a lot of money selling insurance, Susan had told me. And he looked like he'd spent half of it on clothes. He wasn't wearing his suit jacket, but the vest and pants were enough to say that the suit had been made for him and probably cost $750. Fat as he was, there was no gap between the vest and the pants.

'I gave that kid every chance,' Kyle said. 'And she threw it in my face.'

His wife said, 'Please, Harry.'

'I worked my ass off, to get us where we are. And she pulls this, after all she's gotten? She pulls this on me? No thanks. I don't have a daughter anymore, you understand?'

His wife said, 'Maybe it was somebody else, Harry.' She was thin with a dark face and wiry black hair cut short. Her features were thin and her face was narrow. She was wearing a pink blouse and pants, and pink shoes. Her eyes were red. I assumed she'd been crying. I didn't blame her. Harry made me feel a little teary myself.

'Mr. Kyle,' Susan said. 'Talk to Spenser. He's an excellent detective. He can find April, bring her home. You can't reject a child simply because she doesn't please you. Let us try.'

'Listen to her, Harry,' his wife said. 'Your own daughter.'

Kyle looked at me. 'Okay, let's hear your pitch,' he said.

'I got no pitch,' I said. 'I just swung by for a charm fix.'

'What's that supposed to mean?' Kyle said.

'Mr. Kyle,' Susan said, 'April could be in serious trouble. If it really was she you saw in the Combat Zone with an older man, it is important to get her out of there.' She looked at me even harder than she had before.

'So what are you crying to me about?' Kyle said. 'You're worried about her, you go get her.'

'Because I need a home to bring her back to, Mr. Kyle.'

'Yeah, you don't mind bringing her back,

3

but you don't want to take her in, do you?'

'Mr. Kyle, she's not my daughter. Whether I wish to take her in, what's more important is that you wish to take her in. Can't you understand that?'

'Hey,' Kyle said, 'I sold nearly two million dollars in life insurance last year, honey. I can understand a lot of things.'

'How much you got on yourself?' I said.

'What's that got to do with anything?' Kyle said.

'If you call Mrs. Silverman honey again, it'll be relevant.'

'What are you, some kind of tough guy?' Kyle said. But he didn't say it with very much starch.

'Yes,' I said. Susan put her hand on my arm and squeezed.

'Mrs. Kyle,' Susan said, 'do you want your daughter back?'

'Yes.' She looked at her husband. 'Yes, but Harry ... I ... Could I get you some coffee? And some cake? And we could sit down and try to ...' She made a flutter with her right hand and stopped talking.

'For crissake, Bunni, nobody wants any goddamn cake.'

'Harry, I just asked,' Mrs. Kyle said.

'Just shut up, will you, and let me handle

4

this.'

I shifted my weight from one foot to the other. I looked at Susan. I could see the anger tightening her face, pinching small commas at the corners of her mouth.

Kyle turned to us, an in-charge guy, and tossed his chin at me. 'How much you charge?' he said.

'To work for you?'

'Yes.'

'Two hundred billion dollars a day.'

Kyle frowned. For a moment he'd felt comfortable, talking price. He knew about price. 'You being a wise guy?'

'Yes,' I said.

'You want the job or not?' Kyle said.

'I would rather spend the rest of my life at a Barry Manilow concert,' I said.

Kyle looked at Susan, 'I don't know what the hell he's talking about,' he said.

Susan looked half mad and half amused. 'He's saying he doesn't want to work for you.'

'Then what the hell did you bring him here for, for crissake?'

'When I came,' I said, 'I didn't know you. Now I do. If I were your kid, I'd run away too.'

Bunni Kyle said, 'Mr. Spenser.'

Susan said, looking at me at full voltage, 'The girl, the girl needs help. Her father is not her fault.'

'Never mind,' Kyle said. 'The hell with him.'

'For me,' Susan said, looking right at me. 'A favor. For me.'

I took in a deep breath. Mrs. Kyle was looking at me. I said to her, 'I'll work for you, Mrs. Kyle.'

'Like hell you will,' Kyle said. 'I'm not paying you a dime to work for anyone.'

'One dollar,' I said to Mrs. Kyle. 'I will work for you for a dollar. I'll find the kid and bring her back to you.'

'Oh, no,' Kyle said. 'No you don't. I say no, I mean no.'

I put my face into his. His breath smelled of martini and peanuts. 'If you don't button it up,' I said with as much control as I had left, 'I am going to hurt you.'

Kyle opened his mouth to speak and looked at me and saw something in my face that made him shut his mouth without speaking. Susan insinuated herself between us.

'Come on, ducky,' she said. 'Let's go find April.' She leaned back against me, pushing me away with her butt. If I hadn't been so

6

mad I'd have enjoyed it. 'I'll call you, Mrs. Kyle, the minute we find her.' Susan backed us toward the door.

Kyle was looking at me, the color of his face deepening to maroon.

'While you're pushing me,' I murmured to Susan, 'with your seat, could you sway back and forth slightly?'

She gave a harder push.

I said in a falsetto voice, 'That's not what I meant.' And we left.

CHAPTER TWO

'He better not go out during the Thanksgiving season,' I said. We were driving in Susan's big red Ford Bronco. It had oversize tires and a low-range option in four-wheel drive. Susan claimed it went through snowstorms and over mountains and gave her a sense that she could conquer winter.

'He is a terrible turkey, isn't he?' Susan said.

'After we find the girl, can I beat him up?'

Susan shook her head.

'Slash his tires?' I said.

'No.'

'Soap his windows?'

Susan turned down her street.

'I'm not surprised she's tricking,' Susan said.

'The kid?'

'Yes, April. I've been trying to salvage . . . no, that's not the right word . . . prevent the wreck she's been heading for since she was in the tenth grade.'

'She's a senior now?'

'Yes, she's scheduled to graduate in June.'

'Besides being the daughter of a major league dildo, what is her problem?'

Susan swung the Bronco into the driveway. 'I don't know, exactly. I only get her end of it. I've had a couple of conferences with her parents, but you can imagine how productive that was.' She killed the headlights and shut off the engine. It dieseled once and was still. We sat in the car in the dark. 'You may have heard it rumored that adolescent children have to reject their parents in order to establish an identity of their own.'

'I've heard that,' I said.

'I imagine you have,' Susan said. 'You're still doing it.'

'I thought it was just boyish high spirits,' I said.

Susan snorted; somehow she made it sound elegant. 'Anyway,' she said, 'in a case like this, where there's a fixed parental expectation and an inflexible parental stance, the rebellion can get to be extreme.'

'Jeez, I thought all guidance counselors did was hand out college catalogs and army recruiting pamphlets.'

Susan laughed quietly in the dark car. 'Actually, what we do most is approve schedules.'

'Old Harry doesn't strike me as a flexible and understanding guy,' I said.

'No,' Susan said, 'he's not. In many ways he's typical of this town. A bit more extreme, a bit more unloving, but essentially he's left a very much different kind of social circumstance, maybe the first generation to go to college or wear a suit to work. They've moved away, people like Harry Kyle. Moved away from the old neighborhood both literally and figuratively. The old rules from that neighborhood don't apply here. Or people like Harry Kyle don't think they do. They don't know the new rules, so they latch on to the conventions of the media and the assumptions of the magazine ads and the situation comedies. They try to be like everyone else, and what makes it so hard is that everyone else is trying to be like them.'

We got out of the car and walked in the dark evening to Susan's back door. It was ten days till Thanksgiving, and the air was cold.

Susan's kitchen was warm and smelled faintly of apples.

She snapped the overhead light on from a switch by the back door. 'Want some supper?'

I was rummaging for beer in the refrigerator. 'Yes,' I said. 'Want me to make it?'

'No,' she said. 'I've got to learn sometime.'

I sat at the kitchen table and drank beer from the bottle. 'Pilsner Urquell,' I said. 'Do you have a rich lover?'

'I thought you'd like to try it.'

I drank some more. 'Yum, yum,' I said.

Susan took some potatoes from a drawer and began peeling them at the sink. 'So,' she said, 'what's wrong with April Kyle, you ask?'

'She doesn't get on with her parents, you answer.'

'Yes,' Susan said. 'Lucky I've got all that Harvard training.' She put the point of her paring knife into a peeled potato and spun it, gouging out the remnant of an eye. 'It's not that what they wanted for her was so bad—it was that it was so inflexible, and she wasn't consulted. They wanted her to be a cheerleader, to work on the yearbook staff, to get good grades, to go out with football captains, to attract a husband they could be proud of.'

I finished my beer and went to the refrigerator and got another. I noticed with a sense of fast enlarging contentment that there were ten more bottles after this one.

'Shouldn't you drink good beer like that from a glass?' Susan said.

'Absolutely,' I said.

Susan finished peeling potatoes. She sliced them and went to the refrigerator and got out a bundle of scallions. 'Where was I?' she said.

'You were telling me how the Kyles wanted their kid to be Doris Day.'

'Yes, and April decided against it. By the time she got to high school and I began to deal with her she was already in among the burnouts. She was smoking grass, forging absentee excuses. According to her file she had her period every two or three days. Grades were bad, she was inattentive and somewhat defiant in class. I assume that all of this caused lots of yelling, and maybe some slapping, at home. She'd be grounded for weeks at a time, and as soon as she got out of the house she'd do it worse.'

'How'd you do with her?'

'I could talk to her.'

'You could talk to Yasser Arafat,' I said, 'and he'd think he was having a nice time.'

'But that's all. I think she liked to come talk with me. It was better than being in class, and it was better than being picked up and driven home after school and made to stay in your room and not watch TV. She seemed to enjoy talking with me. But I don't think I had any influence on her behavior at all.' She was chopping the scallions. 'Then two weeks ago she dropped out of school and yesterday her mother came to me for help.'

'Who do I talk to?' I said.

'I'll take you over and introduce you to the local police.' Susan put the chopped scallions in another bowl. 'They can give you some information, I suppose. And the burnouts— there's a kid named Hummer ... real name is Carl Hummel, but no one calls him that. He went with her, sort of, and he's ... leader is too strong a word, but he's the most important kid in her circle.'

Susan broke six eggs into a bowl and whipped them up with a fork. She put one dash of Tabasco sauce into the eggs, and two tablespoons—she measured—of my beer.

'Hummer a bad kid?' I said.

She poured a little oil in a fry pan and put the potatoes and scallions in. 'Depends on your definition,' she said. 'By the standards you and Hawk are used to, he's Rebecca of Sunnybrook Farm. But for Smithfield, he's pretty bad.' The potatoes began to sizzle in the pan. 'Would you pour me a little wine, please, cutie pie?'

'Sure,' I said. 'You shouldn't add the scallions at the same time you do the potatoes. By the time the potatoes are done the scallions will be burned.'

Susan smiled at me. 'Why don't you take a flying fuck at a rolling donut,' she said.

I handed her the wine. 'Do I hear you saying you can get on okay without my instruction?' I said.

She stirred the potatoes and scallions around with a spatula.

'Only your body,' she said, 'is indispensable.'

'Everyone tells me that,' I said.

'I assume you can find April,' Susan said.

'Does a cat have an ass?' I said.

'Ah, the poetry of it,' Susan said, 'the pure pleasure of your discourse.'

'But,' I said.

'Yes,' Susan said, 'I know. But once you

find her, then what?'

'I would guess that if she'll come home with me, she won't stay.'

'I don't know,' Susan said. 'It depends on too many things. On what her options are, how bad it has been in Boston. How bad it is at home. Perhaps if you bring her back she'll run away to someplace better.'

'There are a lot of places better,' I said, 'than Harry Kyle's house.'

Susan and I ate her potato and scallion omelet and drank two bottles of Great Western champagne with it. The scallions were a little overcooked, but I managed to down two portions and four hot biscuits that Susan had made from a package.

'Domestic champagne,' I said.

'I don't use Dom Pérignon as a table wine,' she said.

'The sparkle from your eyes is all I need, honey bunny,' I said.

'How much trouble is she in,' Susan said, 'if she really is a streetwalker?'

'In terms of whores,' I said, 'it's unskilled labor, the pay is lousy, the clientele is not top drawer. You gotta turn a lot of tricks to make any money, and a pimp usually takes most of it.'

'Is she in physical danger?'

14

'Sure.' I buttered another biscuit and put on a small dab of boysenberry jam. 'It's not inevitable, but some of your clients could be uncivilized.'

Susan sipped at her champagne. We were eating in the kitchen, but Susan had put candles on the table, and the moving light from them made her face seem animated even in repose. It was the most interesting face I'd ever seen. It never looked quite the same, as if the planes of it shifted minutely after each expression—even when she slept she seemed to radiate force.

'However gratifying it may be to flaunt at her parents,' Susan said, 'ultimately it must make you feel like somebody's rag toy.'

'I imagine,' I said.

'The best we can do is find her,' Susan said. 'Once we've done that, we'll worry about what to do with her.'

'Okay.'

'You shouldn't do it for nothing.'

I shrugged. 'Maybe she can split her earnings with me,' I said.

CHAPTER THREE

I was sitting in the front seat of a Smithfield patrol car talking to a cop named Cataldo. We were cruising along Main Street with the windshield wipers barely keeping up with a cold, hard rain. As he drove, Cataldo's eyes moved back and forth from one side to the other. It was always the same, I thought—big cities, little towns—cops were cops, and when they'd been cops for very long, they looked both ways all the time.

'Kid's hot stuff,' Cataldo said. 'Queen of the burnouts. I've hauled her home four, five times now, puking drunk. Usually the old lady will take her in and clean her up and get her into bed so the old man won't know.'

'During the day?'

'Sometimes—sometimes middle of the afternoon, sometimes later at night. Sometimes one of us will find her on some back road five miles from anywhere and pick her up and bring her home.'

'She get left?' I said.

Cataldo slowed and looked at a parked car and then moved on. 'She never says, but I'd say so. Some guys pick her up in the old

16

man's car, take her for a ride, get their ashes hauled, and drop her off.'

'Guys?'

'Yeah, sure—queen of the gang bang, that's old April.'

'She always drunk?' I said.

Cataldo took a right. 'Nope. Sometimes she's stoned. Sometimes she's neither, sometimes she's just god-damned crazy,' he said.

'High on life.'

'Yeah.'

The houses on either side of the street were set among trees and their yards were broad. In the driveways were Volvo station wagons and Volkswagen Rabbits, here and there a Mercedes sedan. Only occasionally a Chevy Caprice or a Buick Skylark. Smithfield was not obsessive about buying American.

'You ever have to bust her?'

Cataldo shook his head. 'I don't think there's a town ordinance against gang bangs. If there is, we don't enforce it. We've brought her in a couple of times for failing to disperse when ordered but, christ, we don't even have a matron full time. Her mother always comes down.'

'How's the kid act when you pick her up?' I said.

Cataldo swung into the curving drive in front of the high school. In the faculty lot to the right I could see Susan's Bronco, looming like a rhinoceros above the Datsuns and Chevettes. The school was mid-sixties red brick, square and graceless. One of the glass doors in the entry had been shattered, and a piece of plywood closed the gap. Susan had moved up from the junior high school when someone retired. *No more eighth graders* she had said at the time, and two years later she showed no regrets. Susan doing high school guidance had always seemed to me like Greta Garbo co-starring with Dean Jones.

'Mostly depends on how drunk or stoned or whatever, you know. If she was drunk she'd be abusive, if she was stoned she'd be sort of quiet and not with it—go-ahead-arrest-me-I-don't-give-a-shit sort of attitude. If she was sober, she'd be sullen and tough and smoke cigarettes in the corner of her mouth.'

'She have any boyfriends?'

Cataldo drove on out of the driveway of the high school and we cruised across the street into a development of high-priced homes.

'April.' He grinned. 'She has several at a time, usually for half an hour in the back seat of Dad's Buick.'

'Besides that?'

He shook his head. 'No. She hangs on the wall with Hummer a lot, but no dating or that crap.' He looked over at me for a moment. 'You got to understand these kids, Spenser. Having a boyfriend just isn't something you ask about kids like her. You know? I mean, she don't go down to the fucking malt shop either.'

'You got a malt shop in this town?'

'No.'

Behind the lifeless November lawns, merged one into the next, the new colonial houses gleamed in the rain, expensive variations of the same architectural plan like the Kyles' furniture on a larger scale, a neighborhood set: grand, functional, costly, neatly organized, and as charming as a set of dentures. It made me think fondly of L.A. In L.A. there was room for lunacy.

'If you were going to look for her, where would you start?' I said.

Cataldo shrugged, 'Boston, I suppose. She's not around town. Or at least I haven't seen her in the last few days. Usually kids take off from here, they go to Boston.'

'Anyplace special?'

'In Boston, how the hell do I know? That's your area, man. I get in maybe twice a year for a Sox game.'

'Why do you think she acts like she does?' I said.

Cataldo laughed. 'Before I got on the cops I worked ten years as a roofer. What the hell do I know about why she acts that way? She's a goddamned creep, like a lot of the kids in this town.'

'How about Hummer and his group—can you get me in touch with them, would they know where she went?'

'I can put you in touch. They won't tell you shit. Hummer's the worst creep in town.'

'Bad kid?'

Again Cataldo shrugged. 'Yeah—bad in the wrong way, you know?'

We turned down a hill and took a right. The rain came steady and cold against the windshield and rattled on the roof of the car. 'When I was a kid we were bad—a lot of guys I grew up with are in the joint. But they were bad for a reason. They stole stuff because they wanted money. Or they got in fights because somebody insulted their sister or made a pass at their girl or came onto their turf, you know? These kids sneak around and break Coke machines and trash the school windows or set fire to some guy's store—for what? Prove how tough they are. Shit.

20

Toughest kid in this town would get his ass kicked by one of the pom-pom girls in East Boston.' He shook his head. 'They don't know how to act. It's like they never learned about how to act, about how a guy is supposed to act.'

We were near the south edge of town now. Across the street a gas station, a bowling alley, and a small cluster of stores. The gas station was one that sold gas only. Correct change or credit cards after 6 P.M. The bowling alley had been converted from something else. There were kids leaning against the front wall under the marquee out of the rain, collars turned up, smoking with cigarettes cupped in their hands.

'The one with the fur collar,' Cataldo said, 'and the boots half laced?'

'Yeah.'

'That's Hummer,' he said.

'Why don't you swing down back and drop me off, and I'll stroll over and talk with him.'

'He'll give you some shit,' Cataldo said. 'Want me along?'

I shook my head. 'My line of work,' I said, 'taking shit.'

Cataldo nodded. 'Me too,' he said.

CHAPTER FOUR

Hummer looked about seventeen. He must have spent a half hour getting his look right before he came downtown to hang out. His pale tan Timberland boots were carefully half laced and the cuffs of the jeans were carefully caught inside the loose uppers. Despite the cold rain, his bombardier jacket was open, the fur collar up, the collar of his plaid shirt turned up inside the jacket collar. There were three other boys and two girls with Hummer. They were all dressed with the same careful pretense of sloppiness. Suburban tough. I always figured I could take a guy wearing eighty-dollar boots and a crocodile on his sweater, but that's probably just a form of prejudice. On the other hand, I was wearing a leather trench coat with epaulets and a belt. I felt like Joel McCrea in *Foreign Correspondent.*

I said, 'You Hummer?'

He looked up at me slowly, took a drag on his cupped cigarette, and said, 'Who wants to know?'

'Now there you go,' I said. 'You've been watching *Starsky and Hutch* again and stealing all their good lines.'

Hummer said, 'Yeah.'

And I said, 'Yeah, you're Hummer? Or yeah, you been watching *Starsky and Hutch?*'

'What's it to you?'

I looked at one of the girls—she was slim and blond and wore high-heeled black boots and tapered jeans and a down vest over a black turtleneck sweater. She had a plaid umbrella folded up, and she leaned on it like a cane. 'This is slow going, isn't it?' I said.

She shrugged and said, 'Maybe.'

Two of the boys looked at each other and snickered. I never cared much for being snickered at. I took a slow breath. 'I'm trying to locate April Kyle—can any of you help me on that?'

'April May,' the girl with the umbrella said.

'April will,' one of the snickerers said, and they all laughed without letting it really out.

'Whyn't you get lost, man?' Hummer said. 'We ain't got nothing to say about April.'

'Hummer,' I said, 'just because you haven't had your growth spurt yet doesn't mean you're too little to hit.'

'You hit me, and my old man will sue your ass,' Hummer said.

'I imagine so,' I said. 'Any of you care if

23

April Kyle's in trouble?'

'What kind of trouble?'

'Grown-up trouble,' I said. 'She's got herself involved with people who will beat her up for a dollar and kill her for five.'

'How do you know?' It was the girl with the umbrella talking.

I thought about it for a minute. April's reputation didn't have anything to lose. 'She's tricking,' I said, 'in the Combat Zone. That means a pimp, that means the real possibility of abuse, maybe dying.'

'I told her she should stop doing it free,' Hummer said.

'You start her hooking?' I said. I was looking straight into his face.

'Hey, man, no way. I just used to kid her, is all. She got into trouble, she done it on her own.'

'You got any idea where she's living?'

'You a cop?' the umbrella girl said.

'I know it's corny as hell,' I said, 'but I'm a private eye. Couldn't you tell by my leather trench coat?'

'How do we know that?' Hummer said.

'Besides the leather trench coat? I could show you my license. One of your buddies could read it to you.'

One of the other boys said, 'Hey, you carry

24

a gun?'

'Knowing I was going to talk with you toughies, I thought I'd better.'

'What kind you got?'

'Smith and Wesson,' I said. 'Detective special.' I'd found a subject that interested them. 'Thirty-eight caliber. Sam Spade autograph model.'

'Hey, lemme see it,' the kid said.

'No. I'm not here to play guns. I'm trying to find out how to get hold of April Kyle.'

'She had a friend in Boston,' the umbrella girl said.

'Hey, I said we're not telling him nothing,' Hummer said. 'That goes for you too, Michelle.'

I took hold of Hummer's upper arm with my right hand and squeezed it. He tried to flex up his biceps to counteract me, but I was much stronger than he was. From the feel of his upper arm a lot of people were.

'Hummer,' I said, 'be quiet.'

He tried to yank his arm away. I tightened the squeeze a little more. The fixed expression of tolerant superiority began to dissolve. What replaced it looked a lot like discomfort.

'What's the friend's name?' I said to Michelle.

'Come on, man,' Hummer said. He pulled at my grip with his free hand.

'You mind if I discuss the name of April's friend?' I said.

He kept working on my grip without much progress. I squeezed a little more.

'Ow, man, shit—you're busting my goddamned arm.'

'You mind if Michelle tells me stuff?'

'No, ow, no, go ahead, man—tell him, Michelle—let go.'

I eased up on the squeeze, but still held his arm.

'Michelle?'

'Amy Gurwitz,' she said. 'She used to live here, but she moved to Boston.'

'Parents move?'

'No, just her. They threw her out.'

'Address?'

'I don't know.'

Hummer was trying to tug his arm loose.

'Anybody else?' I said.

All of them were silent. The arm squeeze had scared them. I had the secret to dealing with the difficult teen years. Violate their civil rights a little. Cause some pain. Bully them a bit. No such thing as a bad boy.

'No other friends?' I said.

They all shook their heads again, except

Hummer, who was still trying to get his arm loose. I let him succeed. All of them were quiet. Hummer sat with his head down, rubbing his arm.

'You think you're pretty tough, huh?' he said. 'Come out and push around a bunch of kids.'

'I am pretty tough, Hummer. But not because I pushed you around. I pushed you around because I had to. There's people can push me around. Nothing to be ashamed of.'

Hummer didn't look up. None of the other kids looked at him. There was nothing else to say. I walked away, back toward the center of town, where I'd left my car. On the way I looked for a puppy to kick.

CHAPTER FIVE

There were seven people called Gurwitz listed in the Boston telephone directory. None of them was Amy. I called all the numbers and none of them ever heard of Amy. There was one Gurwitz listed in the Smithfield book. I called them. Mrs. Gurwitz didn't know where Amy lived, and didn't know her phone number, and hadn't heard from her since she had left and didn't want to.

'I got three others to think about, mister,' she told me on the phone. 'And the farther away she stays from them, the better I'll like it. Her sister made honor roll last quarter.'

'Any of the kids know how to get in touch with her?'

'They'd better not, and you better not get them involved with her again either.'

'No, ma'am,' I said. 'Thank you for your time.' I hung up and called Susan at the high school.

'The name Amy Gurwitz mean anything to you?' I said.

'Yes. She dropped out last year.'

'She and April are supposed to be friends.'

'Could be. They were both sort of lost, alone kids. I don't know.'

'She got any siblings in the high school?'

'I think a sister, Meredith.'

'I talked to Amy's mom. She doesn't know Amy's whereabouts and doesn't want to. Maybe you could ask the kid sister. She must be smart. She made honor roll last quarter.'

'I'll talk with her,' Susan said, 'and call you back. Are you at my house?'

'Yeah, you know the number?'

She hung up. I leaned my forearms on the

kitchen table and looked out the window. The maple trees were black and slick in the rain, their bare branches shiny. The flower bed was a soggy matting of dead stems. The house was so still you could hear its vital functions. The furnace cycling on and then off as the thermostat required. The faint movement of air from the heat vents. The periodic click, somewhere, probably of the gas meter. I had listened to too much silence in my life. As I got older I didn't get to like it more.

A barrel-bodied Labrador retriever nosed through Susan's backyard, its tail making a steady arc as it foraged for anything that might have been left for the birds. There was nothing there, but she showed no sign of discouragement and moved on past the naked forsythias and into the next yard, with her tail making its rhythmical sweeping wag.

The phone rang. Susan said, 'Okay. Meredith Gurwitz doesn't know where her sister is, but she's got a phone number where she can reach her. You got a pencil?'

'Yes.'

'Okay, here it is,' Susan said, and read me the number. 'Can you find the address from the number?'

'You forget to whom you speak,' I said.

29

'I withdraw the question,' Susan said.

'Before I hang up,' I said, 'tell me something.'

'Yes?'

'Do you spend much time at work fantasizing about my nude body?'

'No.'

'Let me rephrase the question,' I said.

'Just see if you can find out the address for the phone number,' Susan said, and hung up. She was probably embarrassed that I'd discovered her secret.

I looked in the phone book and then dialed the telephone business office in Government Center and asked for my service representative.

The operator said, 'May I have your telephone number, sir?'—they never said *phone* at telephone business offices. I gave her the mystery number. She said, 'I'll connect you,' and in a moment a female voice said, 'Mrs. Foye. May I help you?'

'You're damned right,' I said. 'This is Mr. Phunuff'—I turned my head and blurred the name—'and I am getting all sorts of mail from you people that doesn't belong to me. What have you got there for an address, anyway?'

'I'm very sorry, Mr. Poitras,' she said.

'What kind of mail are you getting?'

'I'm getting the kind I don't want and I'm about damned ready to call the DPU. Now what the hell kind of address have you got for me?'

'We have you at Three Sixty Beacon Street, Mr. Poitras.'

'Yeah, that's right,' I said, mollified, 'and you got my named spelled right? P-O-I-T-R-A-S?'

'Yes, that's what we have—Mitchell Robert Poitras.'

'Well, then, how come I'm getting all this stuff in the mail?'

'Sir, if you could just tell me what exactly you are getting . . . ?'

'Yeah, right, well, look—Mrs. Foye, is it?—here's what I'll do. I'll package it up and send it all to you. Are you in Government Center?'

'Yes. Six Bowdoin Square.'

'Well, I'll send it in and you'll see for yourself.'

'If you'd . . .' and I hung up. Mitchell Poitras, 360 Beacon Street. I probably could have got Cataldo to get the address for me, or Frank Belson in Boston, but it's always good to know you can still do it on your own if you need to. It was a lot better than bullying a

31

seventeen-year-old kid. Ma Bell was a worthy opponent.

Three Sixty Beacon would be somewhere around Fairfield or Gloucester. Condos: walnut paneling, skylights, private gardens, deeded parking, working fireplaces, gourmet kitchens. Amy had not lowered her standard any by moving in with Mitchell Poitras.

It was raining harder as I drove into Boston. The convertible roof on my MG was aging and some of the snaps were gone. Water leaked inoffensively around the snapless gaps and trickled amiably down the doorframe. Might as well save Amy Gurwitz, too, while I was in the neighborhood. They could make honor roll together. I couldn't ever remember making honor roll. Probably why my roof leaked.

CHAPTER SIX

There are few city places handsomer than Back Bay, Boston. The long rows of brick town houses with their idiosyncratic rooflines and their black iron fences out front marched along the dead-flat landfill streets from the Common to Kenmore Square in parallel with the river. There were brownstone fronts, and occasionally gray granite fronts, and, rarely, marble fronts. But the dominant impression of these three- and four- and five-story contiguous buildings was red brick, softened by age and glazed with the cold November rain. There were trees and shrubs, and flower beds in the minuscule front yards. They were somber and wet now, but on summer days they frolicked with color and growth. Even in a cold wet rain, with the day getting darker, it was very nice there. Almost all the dog droppings were in the gutter.

Three sixty was just past Fairfield, on the left, with a low wrought-iron picket fence and a gate. What was probably a magnolia tree stood in dark outline waiting for the spring. Three granite steps led to the doorway. There were double glass doors, and past them a small foyer with flagstone floor and a white wooden door with raised panels. I rang.

Water dripped off the slate roof three stories up. The inside door opened and a woman looked at me through the glass of the outer doors. She wore an ankle-length long-sleeved black dress with white fur cuffs and white fur at the collar. Her hair was blonder than a lemon and done in a mass of curls that overpowered her small face. Her nails were painted red, her eyes were shadowed, her lips were glossy crimson. She had large rings on each finger of each hand. The ringless thumbs seemed underdressed. As she stepped toward me her split skirt fell apart, showing high black boots with very high spiked heels. She opened one of the glass doors.

'Yes?'

Her face was startling. The rest of her was so noisy that you didn't pay much attention to her face until your nerves calmed a little. Up close her face was maybe sixteen years old. Behind the eye shadow and mascara and lip gloss and blusher and things I didn't know the name of was a barely formed sixteen-year-old face. She smiled inquiringly when she said *yes* and I noticed she had a space between her front teeth.

I said, 'My name's Spenser. I'm looking for Amy Gurwitz.'

'Why do you want to see her?' the girl said. Her voice went with her face. It was a voice for saying, *Oh, wow!* and *Far out!* It was a voice to be raised in praise of rock musicians. She spoke carefully with her little voice, and slowly, as if nothing she said came easy to her.

'Because her friend, April Kyle, is in some

trouble, and I'm trying to find April so I can help her.'

'Oh.'

The rain continued to drip off the roof, splashing into a puddle that had formed in the hard dirt where the base of the granite steps met the foundation of the house. The girl bit her lower lip, moving her lower jaw so that the lip scraped slowly across the edge of her top teeth. When it scraped free, she did it again.

Finally, after cycling the lower lip past the upper teeth five or six times, she said, 'Won't you come in, please?'

I said, 'Thank you,' and in we went.

There was a hallway with stairs along the left wall leading up. A door on the right wall, another door past the stairs. A large oil painting with romanticized mountains in it hung on the wall next to the right-hand door. The only other thing in the hall was a brass umbrella stand with maybe five umbrellas in it. They didn't look as if they'd ever been used. They were for show. Like a breast-pocket hankie.

We went straight back past the stairs and through the door at the end of the hall. Then down three stairs to the living room. At the far end of the living room French doors opened out onto a patio. On the right-hand wall a large marble-faced fireplace, above it another picture of purple mountains' majesty. In the left corner was a bar, directly beside the step down, and in between the bar and the French doors were several beige armchairs and a large beige couch. The walls were beige, the carpet was beige. The woodwork was walnut.

'Won't you sit down?' She gestured carefully at the sofa.

'Thank you.' I sat on the sofa.

'Would you care for a drink?'

Was it legal for a child to serve beer to a consenting adult in the privacy of her home? What if the Alcoholic Beverage Commission had the place bugged? There was one way to find out.

'I'll take a beer if you have one,' I said.

If she was an agent, undercover for ABC, I could claim entrapment.

'Certainly,' she said. 'Excuse me.' She walked behind the bar and bent over. I heard a door open. She stood up with a bottle of Molson Golden Ale. She found an opener, popped the top, reached under her bar, came up with a beer mug, poured the beer into the glass, taking her time, trying to get the whole bottle into the mug without overflowing the foam. When she had it full to the brim and the bottle was empty, she put the bottle out of sight, put the mug on a little walnut tray, and brought it to me. From a drawer in the coffee table she took out a coaster, put the coaster in front of me, and carefully put the beer on the coaster. She smiled again and then brought the tray back and put it out of sight behind the bar. She then came back and sat down in one of the armchairs across from me and crossed her legs, smoothing her skirt over her thighs.

'I am Amy Gurwitz,' she said.

I picked up my beer mug, carefully so as not to spill, and took a small sip. I didn't dare guzzle it—she'd think she had to get me another one and that would kill the afternoon.

'Do you know where April Kyle is?' I said.

She frowned slightly, and I knew she was trying to think. 'May I ask why you wish to know?' Amy said. Her hands were folded still in her lap. She had her head tilted delicately so that she seemed to be looking down over her cheekbones at me. Elegant.

'Her parents think she's become a prostitute, and they are worried about her.'

'You a cop . . . policeman?'

'I am a private detective,' I said.

She raised her eyebrows and smiled. 'Oh, isn't that interesting.'

I nodded and sipped a little more beer. She smiled at me.

'Are you thinking?' I said.

'Excuse me?'

'Are you thinking about my question?'

'Oh. . . . No.'

'Can you put me in touch with April? Do you know where she is?'

She smiled again, the apex of courtesy. 'No, I'm terribly sorry. I don't know where April is.'

I didn't get a ring of sincerity in her voice. Or insincerity. I didn't hear the ring of anything in her voice. She was like a kid playacting. Playing grown-up. She offered me a filter-tipped cigarette from a box on the coffee table. I said, 'No, thank you.'

She said, 'Do you mind if I smoke?'

I said, 'No.'

She lit her cigarette with a big silver table lighter.

'Would you have any ideas on where I might look for April?' I said.

Amy held her cigarette carefully out near the fingertips of her index and middle fingers. She inhaled and exhaled, carefully blowing the smoke away from me. 'Gracious,

I really couldn't say. I haven't seen April since I moved from Smithfield.'

I nodded. 'You think she might be a whore?' I said.

'Oh, I hope not. She was always so nice. I don't think she'd do that.'

'Do you live here with Mitchell Poitras?'

She smiled and shook her head vaguely. It was neither a negative nor affirmative movement—it was something in between, an avoidance gesture.

'Do you work?'

'I'm at home just now,' she said. Her eyes were shallow and meaningless as she spoke. Her smile was polite. She looked like a Barbie doll.

'So who pays the rent?'

She made her vague head movement again and smoked some more of her cigarette.

'What does Mitchell do for a living?' I said.

She looked up at the clock. 'I really must be starting my dinner pretty soon. I'm afraid you'll have to excuse me.' She stood. I was being outclassed by a sixteen-year-old girl. Should I give her the famous Spenserian arm squeeze? Or I could shoot her.

I said, 'Okay, thanks for your time.' I took a card from my shirt pocket and gave it to her. 'If you should hear from April, could you give me a call?'

She put the card on the coffee table and walked in stately cadence to the door and opened it. She smiled. I smiled. I went out. She shut the door. I turned up my coat collar and walked to my car. The small rain still fell.

CHAPTER SEVEN

I was not happy. I had learned so little from Amy Gurwitz that I felt as if I'd gotten stupider while I was in there. It wasn't so much that I suspected her of lying. I had no sense at all of her or her reactions. It bothered me. She seemed in some ways the full realization of what a sixteen-year-old kid would imagine adult sophistication to be. Like a cartoon of a rich Back Bay matron. But that's all she was. There was no fun in her, no pleasure in the game. No showing off. No rebellion. No flirtation. And she was living with some guy old enough to have amassed the bundle it had cost for that town house. None of it was right. I didn't like it. I had the feeling that maybe she didn't care if I liked it.

I looked at my watch—after four. I was hungry. I left my car where it was and walked over to the Cafe Vendome on Commonwealth and had a cheeseburger and three beers. When I got through it was 5:05. With the rain still coming I walked down Commonwealth and across the Common and on into the Combat Zone at the foot of Boylston Street. It was twenty-five to six when I got there. But that didn't matter. Time stood still in the Combat Zone. You could see a dirty movie or a quarter peep show at most hours of the day or night. You could purchase a skin magazine specialized for almost every peculiarity. You could get a drink. Fellatio. Pizza by the slice, adult novelty items. Everything necessary to sustain the human spirit. The neon lights and oversized flashing bulbs and crudely drawn signs that advertised all of this and much more (*All Live Acts! Nude College Girls!*) were plastered onto old commercial buildings, some of them once elegant in the red brick and brownstone that Boston had been built in. Above the one-story glitz of the Combat Zone the ornamental arched windows and the intricate rooflines of the old buildings were as incongruous as a nun at a stag film.

I moved along lower Washington Street with my hands in my pockets, trying to look like a guy from Melrose whose wife was away till Thursday. Except for the Back Bay, Boston's streets are routinely narrow and twisted. Washington Street where it descends into the Combat Zone is notably so. Cars cruised slowly by. Often they were filled with young men drinking beer from the bottle and yelling out the window at women. Sailors from other countries, women in suggestive clothes, men in stretch fabric suits and miracle fabric raincoats with epaulets and belts, an elderly Oriental man moving through on his way to Chinatown, seeming oblivious of the crudely packaged lust about him. Winos shuffled about down here too, and kids wearing black warm-up jackets with yellow leather sleeves that said Norfolk County Champs 80–81 in the center of a large yellow football on the left front.

I had April Kyle's picture in my inside pocket, but I didn't need it. I'd studied it. I knew what she looked like. At least, I knew what she looked like when she'd had it taken for graduation. The Combat Zone look was a little different. I hadn't seen a cashmere sweater or a pair of Top-Siders down here in some time.

Two girls came out of a bar ahead of me. One was black, one was white. They both wore blond wigs. They both had on slit skirt evening gowns with sequins and cleavage. The white girl wore open-toed sling-back high heels. The black girl had on boots. Both wore transparent plastic raincoats with transparent hoods up over their wigs. The white girl was smoking a joint. I smiled at them as they came toward me.

'Hi, girls,' I said. 'What's happening?'

The black girl said to her friend, 'Now, he ain't no cop, is he?'

The white girl said, 'Oh, no. He's a dentist probably from Cow Hampshire.'

The black girl said, 'Bullshit,' making it a four-syllable phrase, and the two of them kept moving. I'd have to work on my suburban look a little.

In the window of a store next to a peep show there was an assortment of leather items. Their uses weren't apparent, but bondage and discipline seemed a good estimate. Two men with crew cuts held hands while they looked in the window beside me. One of them had on a black motorcycle jacket. The other wore a black turtle-neck jersey and a down vest. Both wore low white sneakers and dark socks. The one in the leather jacket nudged the other one and whispered something. They both giggled, and I moved on.

Rock music with a heavy thumping drive racketed out of the bars and strip joints, the multicolored neon reflected from the shiny streets and rain-polished windows, someone blared his automobile horn insistently, between two parked cars a man vomited while another man in a long blue overcoat held him around the waist to keep him from pitching forward. In the window of an adult bookstore there was a collection of magazines devoted to naked children of both sexes, hairless and innocent, wearing makeup.

A thought occurred to me that had not occurred before. What was Harry Kyle doing in the Zone when he'd seen his daughter? Selling clap insurance? Catching the Harry Reems retrospective at the Pussycat Cinema? I'd never fallen under the spell of the Combat Zone. I was in favor of female nudity, but the Zone left me with the queasy feeling I used to get when I smoked first thing in the morning on an empty stomach. I had quit smoking in 1962, but I could still remember it clearly. The pack of Camels in the shirt pocket, the first drag with coffee after breakfast, the days in Korea when we'd take a break and light

44

up, the automatic gesture I always made leaving the house of patting my chest to make sure I had cigarettes, the satisfied feeling when I did, like having money in your wallet. Now when I left the house I patted my hip to check the gun.

A silver-gray Buick Electra pulled up to the curb near me and a black woman in a lavender jump suit got out. The Buick pulled away and the woman stepped into the doorway of a pinball arcade out of the rain. The pants of the jump suit were tucked into the tops of black suede boots with very high heels. She wore no coat and she shivered as she stood in the doorway. A middle-sized black man with long arms got out of a white Jaguar sedan parked at the curb and joined her in the doorway. She gave him something and he put it in his pocket. I went over to the doorway and stood beside them. The woman's hair was in a silver-tipped natural. She had prominent teeth and her lipstick was the same shade of lavender as her jump suit. There was a small, new moon scar beside her left eye. The man's nose was flat and broad. He had a mustache trimmed thin and high cheekbones that made him look Oriental. He was wearing a white cowboy hat with a peacock feather and white leather trench coat

45

with the collar turned up and the belt knotted in the front, the big gold buckle dangling free beyond the knot. I said, 'Excuse me, I'm looking for a girl—maybe you could help.'

The black man eyed me. The woman looked at him.

'What'd you have in mind, man?' he said.

I took April's picture out of my pocket and showed it to them. 'Her,' I said.

The man looked at the picture in the light that spilled out of the arcade. He shook his head. 'Ain't one of mine,' he said. 'What's your interest? I mean, I know some girls just as good if your taste runs that way.'

'Nope,' I said. 'I want to find her.'

The man grinned. 'Figured you wasn't no tourist,' he said. 'Cop?'

I said to the woman, 'How about you?' I showed her the picture. 'You ever see her?'

'She don't know nothing,' the man said.

I ignored him. I looked at he woman. She shrugged. The man moved more fully between us. 'I say she don't know nothing,' he said. 'She don't talk. I talk.' His shoulders were sloping and the neck that showed at the open collar of his coat was thick and muscular.

'I noticed that,' I said.

'You fucking with me, man,' he said. His

dark eyes gleamed at me.

'Not me,' I said. 'I'm just looking for this little girl.'

'How come?'

'Parents want her home,' I said.

'They think she around here?'

'Yeah.'

'And they don't like their little sweetie giving blow jobs in the back seat of some John's car?' he said.

'Yeah.'

'Ain't our problem,' he said.

'No. It's mine,' I said.

'They paying you?' he said. The woman stood motionless, hugging herself, shivering, paying attention only to the black man. Like an attentive dog. That's probably where she got the scar near her eye. Obedience training.

'Yes.'

'Whyn't they come to look for her themselves? I had a kid run off, I'd go get her myself. I wouldn't waste money on some shoofly.'

'Too busy, probably,' I said. 'Maybe too scared. Guys like you would scare them.'

'I don't scare you?' he said.

'Not very much,' I said.

He grinned and took his hands out of his coat pockets. In the right hand was a brown

47

leather sap. He tapped his palm with it. I reached out with my left hand and snapped it away from him.

'Reflexes,' I said. 'You spend your time pushing around drunken high school kids and your reflexes go.'

He looked at me with his eyes half shut. I was about three inches taller than he was and he had to look up slightly. Never an asset.

'Quick,' he said. He looked at the woman. 'See? I told you he ain't no tourist.' As he talked he was absently untying his belt that held his trench coat closed.

I said, 'If you open that coat I will clean your teeth with your sap.'

He was indignant. 'What's the matter with you, man?' he said.

'If you got a piece,' I said, 'it's dumb to keep it buttoned up under your coat.'

He looked at my coat. It was hanging open. 'I got no piece, man,' he said.

'I do,' I said. 'And now I got a blackjack too.'

'You asking for a lot of trouble, Jim.'

'I can handle a lot of trouble,' I said. If only I still smoked. A line like that needs cigarette smoke curling around it. 'While we're waiting for it to start, why don't you take a walk?'

'You keeping the sap?' he said.

'I'm going to count five. If you're still here, I'm going to rattle your face with it.'

He raised his hands slightly, 'All right, man. All right, be cool.' He jerked his head at the woman.

'No,' I said. 'Just you.'

He put one hand out to take the woman's arm. I flicked the blackjack out and tapped him on the forearm. It was a light tap, but the weighted head of the thing would make his arm go numb.

'One,' I said. 'Two.'

He turned and walked down the street away from us.

There was no expression on the woman's face. She still hugged herself and shivered. 'He ain't gonna let you roust him like that,' she said.

'I think he just did.'

She shook her head. 'Nope. He gotta be first man. Specially in front of one of his girls. He be back.'

'You know the girl,' I said.

'What's the difference?'

'I'm worried about her. She's sixteen and tricking in the Zone.'

'Little blond honky do it, everybody gets worried. How come you ain't worried about me?'

'Nobody hired me to worry about you,' I said. 'You want to retain me?'

'I seen her around,' the woman said. 'Suburb pussy.'

'Who's her pimp?'

She shrugged again. 'Red, maybe?'

'Red got a last name?'

'I don't know. White dude, red hair.'

'Coincidence,' I said.

'Huh?'

'Never mind. Where's Red hang out?'

'Bar called The Slipper, down toward Boylston.'

'I know where it is. You want my coat?'

She shook her head. 'Trumps don't let us wear none,' she said. 'Say it's not sexy.'

'Trumps? The guy I just talked with?'

She nodded. 'You better remember it. You gonna see him again, you hang around here.'

I held the blackjack out to her. 'Here. When you see him give this back to him.'

She shook her head. 'Naw. He gonna be mad enough. I gotta take a beating now. I don't want to make him madder.'

'What's he going to beat you up for?'

''Cause I seen you roust him.'

The water dripped off the doorway canopy like a beaded curtain. A trio of sailors pushed past us in the doorway and went into the arcade. They all wore peacoats with the collars up.

I said, 'You want to come with me?'

She looked straight at me for the first time. 'Come with you?' She laughed. Derision. 'Come with you? And do what? You gonna marry me? Take me away from all this?'

'I could take you someplace where Trumps wouldn't beat you up.'

The laugh again. As mirthless as a knife blade. 'People been beating me up all my life, man. One more won't hurt.'

I nodded.

She smiled slightly. 'Get lost. There's nothing you can do for me. You don't know nothing about it. Just get out of here 'fore Trumps gets back, maybe with help, and blows you away. There's nothing you can do for me.'

'You want any money?' I said.

'The honky solution to everything,' she said. 'Keep it. You give it to me and Trumps take it away. Just get out of here. And watch your back.'

I nodded again. 'So long,' I said.

'Yeah,' she said.

I walked up through Chinatown, came out on Tremont, turned right, and the Zone was behind me. I crossed Tremont at Boylston and started across the Common toward Beacon. They were starting to put up the Christmas displays on the Common.

There weren't many people in the Common, and the rain still came steady, but not very hard. We were maybe five degrees from a snowstorm. The falling rain made the lights in the city around the Common haze a bit and soften. The rain also made the air seem clean, and it muffled the sound of traffic on Tremont Street and Charles Street. It was still and wet. A cop sat on a barrel-chested sorrel horse near the wading pool. He had on a glistening yellow slicker. There was a damp horse smell as I passed them. I liked it. When I was small there were a lot of horses around. They pulled the trash wagons and the milk carts. There was always horse manure in the streets. When Emerson and Whitman had strolled across this Common speaking of 'Leaves of Grass,' there were horses abounding—dignified and symmetrical with a pleasant odor.

CHAPTER EIGHT

I parked down from Amy Gurwitz's town house on Beacon between Exeter and Fairfield. I had to ride around the block for nearly an hour until a space cleared. The morning was clear and bright and the sun made stark shadows along the small bare trees in the tiny front yards along the street. I had a Thermos of coffee and a bag of corn muffins that I'd bought, recently made at a Dunkin' Donuts shop on Boylston Street. Say what you will about their architecture, Dunkin' Donuts makes a fine corn muffin. I ate one with some coffee.

I didn't figure that April Kyle would be working the streets at 9:30 in the morning. Susan was in school. I'd already run my five miles along the river. The Ice Age art exhibit had departed the Science Museum. I'd read *The New Yorker*. Only an animal would lift weights at this hour. I was reading *Sartoris* that month, but I'd left it at Susan's. The Ritz Bar didn't open until 11:30. Why not sit around and look at the Gurwitz place? There was nothing else to do.

Looking at Amy's place wasn't much to

do. Nobody came out. On the other hand, nobody went in, either. The closest I came was when an elderly woman in a long black Persian lamb coat walked two animals past Amy's steps. I assumed they were dogs, though the size and look of them suggested a pair of pet rats on a leash, wearing little bitty plaid sweaters. I ate another corn muffin, drank some more coffee. The mailman went by. I tilted the seat back and slouched a little more. I crossed my arms on my chest. After a while I uncrossed them. Always self-amusing. Never without resources.

A little after two in the afternoon a brown Chevrolet Caprice wagon pulled up in front of Amy's place and double parked. Three young women got out and went in to Amy's foyer and didn't come out. The Caprice pulled away.

About 2:20 a man in a tweed sport coat and a long muffler walked down Fairfield Street from Commonwealth, turned left, and mounted Amy's stairs. He went in. I finished my coffee. At three a very fat guy appeared out of the alley that ran behind Amy's place and walked down Fairfield and went toward the town house. As he walked he sorted keys on a key ring. He went up the stairs and disappeared. The afternoon edged by.

Nobody else went in. Nobody at all came out. Were they all visiting Amy? There was no other tenant in the three-story building. I'd noticed that yesterday. One mailbox, one buzzer, one entrance. So they were at least visiting Amy's place. The guy with the key was probably Poitras. Three young women, girls really, and one guy older than that, and Poitras. So what? Amy had some little chums over to listen to her Devo records and some guy had stopped by to see Poitras, who was a little late. None of the girls was April Kyle. So why was it my business? I looked at my watch. It was quarter to five. I had to meet Hawk at five. I looked at Amy's town house again. No clue appeared. There'd be other slow days. It could be my hobby. Like collecting baseball cards or old campaign buttons. In my spare time I'd come over and stare at Amy Gurwitz's doorway. It's good to keep busy.

I cranked up the MG, took a left on Gloucester, and headed for Copley Square. Hawk was standing outside the Copley Plaza Hotel wearing a glistening black leather jacket and skintight designer jeans tucked into black cowboy boots that glistened like the jacket. He was a little over 6 feet 2 inches, maybe an inch taller than I was, and weighed about two hundred. Like me. He blended with the august Bostonian exterior of the Copley Plaza like a hooded cobra. People glanced covertly at him, circling slightly as they passed him, unconsciously keeping their distance. He wore no hat and his smooth black head was as shiny as his jacket and boots.

I pulled the MG in beside him at the curb and he got in.

'This thing ain't big enough for either one of us,' he said. 'When you getting something that fits?'

'It goes with my preppy look,' I said. 'You get one of these, they let you drive around the north shore, watch polo, anything you want.'

I let the clutch in and turned right on Dartmouth.

'How you get laid in one of these?' Hawk said.

'You just don't understand preppy,' I said. 'I know it's not your fault. You're only a couple of generations out of the jungle. I realize that. But if you're preppy you don't get laid in a car.'

'Where you get laid if you preppy?'

I sniffed. 'One doesn't,' I said.

'Preppies gonna be outnumbered in a while,' Hawk said. 'Where we going?'

I took April Kyle's picture out of my pocket and showed it to Hawk.

'We're going to eat dinner and then we're going to look for her,' I said.

'What we gonna do when we find her?'

'I don't know,' I said. 'Urge her to go home, I guess.'

'What you paying?'

'Half my fee,' I said, 'and expenses.'

'How much you getting?'

'A buck,' I said.

'You paying for dinner?' Hawk said.

'Yeah.'

'Better be a big meal.'

CHAPTER NINE

'You want somebody killed,' Hawk said, 'you gotta give me the whole dollar.'

'I like a man with standards,' I said.

We were walking on Washington Street toward Boylston. As we moved along people got out of the way, spilling to each side of Hawk the way water surges past the prow of a cruiser. No one mistook him for a cop. The night was pleasant, not very cold, and the streets in the Combat Zone were crowded.

'Who this pimp I supposed to keep off your back?' Hawk said.

'Name's Trumps,' I said. 'Black, middle-sized, long arms, drives a white Jag sedan. Looks like he works out. You know him?'

Hawk stopped and looked at me. 'Trumps,' he said. 'I wish I see you take that sap away.' He smiled, and his face looked joyful.

'Bad?' I said.

'Oh, yeah—he bad, all right. He almost as bad as he think he is.'

'Bad as you?' I said.

Hawk's face looked even more cheerful, the glistening smile even wider. 'Course not,' he said. 'Nobody as bad as me. Except maybe you, and you too softhearted.'

We moved on again. Hawk paid no attention to the merchandise. He looked at the people.

'Trumps operate independently,' I said, 'or is he part of a chain?'

'Chain,' Hawk said. 'Works for Tony Marcus.'

'The regent of Roxbury,' I said.

Hawks shrugged.

'You know Tony?' I said.

'Sure,' Hawk said. 'Done a little work for him here and there.' He grinned. 'Security and enforcement division. He pay better than you.'

'Yeah, but does he have a nice personality?'

Ahead of us, at the corner of Boylston and Washington, was a bar with a large flashing sign that said, THE SLIPPER. The sign was made up of individual white light bulbs, and they flickered on and off in a random sequence and gave the effect of strobe lighting in a disco.

Hawk said, 'Now we're not looking for Trumps around here, right?'

'Right, we're looking for a white guy named Red. Or the kid in the picture, or both. Our only interest in Trumps is to keep him from blowing me up,' I said.

We went into the club. It was crowded and dark and loud. Behind the bar three naked young women danced in a pink light. Danced is probably too strong. I'd been to see Paul Giacomin in a couple of jazz dance recitals and my dance aesthetics were becoming polished. Some of the customers were watching closely; others paid no attention at all. Hawk and I pushed among the crowd looking for Red. A bar girl asked us to buy her a drink. I said no. She started to argue, and Hawk looked at her and she stopped and went away. It took maybe another minute before one of the bouncers picked up that we weren't here for the nudies or the booze. He eased over to us.

'You fellas looking for something?' he said, sort of politely. He was a bulky kid, probably a football player from Northeastern or B.C., wearing a white turtleneck sweater and a maroon sports jacket. Hawk looked faintly amused.

'Guy named Red,' I said. 'Somebody told me he hung out here.'

The kid gestured at the room, dense with people and noise. 'Lots of people hang out here.'

'Red's a pimp,' I said.

The kid made a spread-hands gesture, palms up. 'You looking for broads?'

'We from the Chamber of Commerce,' Hawk said. 'We here to give Red a Junior Achievement award.'

The kid stared at Hawk. Hawk smiled at him.

'Any minimum here?' I said.

'Ten bucks,' the kid said.

I gave him a twenty. He folded it in half and then half again and put it in the breast of his maroon blazer. He made a little traffic-stopping gesture about waist high with his left hand. 'No trouble,' he said.

'None at all,' I said.

At the bar nearby a man wearing horn-rimmed glasses yelled at one of the dancing girls, 'Can you pick up a quarter with that thing?'

'No,' she said. 'Can you with yours?'

'Maybe not,' the man yelled, 'but I can bat 'em around a little.'

He laughed and looked around the bar. The bouncer nodded at us and moved toward him. I looked at the girl dancing. Her face was blank as she stared out into the dark room.

Hawk said, 'I circle around this way. You go that way. Meet you in the middle.'

I nodded, and pushed toward the dark booths along the right-hand wall. In the second one I found Red. He was sitting alone in a booth for four, wearing his overcoat and drinking coffee. The overcoat was gray with black velvet lapels. His hair was red, and it had receded back sharply on each side, leaving a keen widow's peak pointing down at his forehead. I slid into the booth opposite him. He looked up from his coffee cup as he took a sip, then put the cup carefully back in the saucer.

'What'll it be?' he said.

His face was white and fat with puffy cheeks. There was some sweat on his upper lip. I showed him my picture of April Kyle. He looked at it and handed it back. 'So,' he said. His voice was very soft, hard to hear in the noisy room.

'Know her?' I said.

'Know a hundred like her,' he said.

'I don't want a hundred like her, I said. 'I'm looking for her.'

'I heard you were,' he said. I found myself leaning forward to hear him.

I nodded. We were quiet. Across the room, above the crowd, a new team of three dancers came on stage. Red drank some more coffee. He held the cup in both hands as he drank, as if it were a bowl, ignoring the handle. He looked past me over the rim of the cup. I looked up. Trumps was there and behind him two other black men. Trumps's coat was unbuttoned.

I looked at Red, 'He the one you heard it from?'

Red nodded.

Trumps said, 'The quiff told me she sent you down here. I was hoping you'd come.'

'Quiff,' I said. 'Trumps, you're a pleasure to listen to. I haven't heard the word *quiff* since Eddie Fisher was big.'

'Never mind the shit, man. Get out of the booth. You got some things to learn.'

Red sipped some more coffee, his pale blue eyes blank as they looked at me. One of the men behind Trumps, a tall man with very square high shoulders, showed me a gun. He held it low, concealed from the room by his body. A Beretta. Expensive. Nothing but the best.

'Come on, smart ass,' Trumps said. 'We going someplace and see how tough you are.'

'You can find that out right now,' I said. 'I'm tough enough not to go.'

'Okay, motherfucker, then we'll do it while you sit there,' Trumps said. His voice was hoarse and intense. He put his hand into his coat pocket and brought out a spring knife and snapped it open. Behind him Hawk appeared and banged together the heads of his two helpers. It sounded like a bat hitting a baseball. Trumps half turned. I caught his knife hand and yanked him toward me, turning the knife away as I did. I put my left hand behind the elbow of his knife arm and bent the arm backward. He grunted with pain. The knife clattered out of his hand onto the table. I pushed him away, picked up the knife, and folded the blade back into the handle. Trumps caught his balance with one

hand on the back of the booth and stared at
Hawk.

Hawk smiled at him that pleasant,
unfeeling smile. 'Evening, Trumps,' Hawk
said. He held the Beretta loosely in his right
hand. Not aimed at anything. Both of the
men whose heads had banged were sunk to
their knees. One leaned his head groggily
against the edge of the table. The other
rocked on his haunches with his hands
clutched behind his head and his forearms
pressing against his temples.

Trumps's voice was choked. 'What you
doing in this, Hawk?'

Hawk nodded at me. 'I with him,' he said.

'The honky?'

'I usually call him Ofay, but yeah, I with
him.'

'Against a brother?'

'Uh-huh.'

Red was silent and still across the booth.
No bouncers came near.

Trumps said, 'I didn't know you in this,
Hawk.'

Hawk smiled and nodded.

'He rousted me in front of one of my
whores,' Trumps said.

'He does that,' Hawk said.

'He got me when I wasn't ready,' Trumps

said.

Hawk smiled. 'Don't matter none,' he said. 'He get you when you're not ready, when you are ready. You a mean little bastard, Trumps, but Spenser's the best around—almost.'

'I didn't know he was with you, Hawk,' Trumps said.

'He is,' Hawk said. He looked at Trumps. Trumps shifted slightly and looked at his switchblade, lying on the table in front of me. Then he looked back at Hawk.

'I didn't know,' he said again.

'He ever get back-shot or something, I know who to look for,' Hawk said.

'Never happen,' Trumps said.

Hawk reached down and yanked both groggy men to their feet. The muscles in his upper arms bunched when he did and stressed the sleeves of his leather jacket.

'Before you go,' I said to Trumps. 'Have you seen that girl I was looking for?'

Trumps didn't look at me. He looked at Hawk the way his whore had looked at him. 'She's one of Red's,' Trumps said. 'She work for Red.'

Hawk nodded. He made a small dismissive gesture with his right hand and Trumps and his helpers left. The helpers were very rocky as they moved through the crowd.

'Ofay?' I said.

'I a real traditional guy,' Hawk said. He put the Beretta into his belt and slid into the booth beside Red. There was more sweat on Red's upper lip, I thought.

'Not too many people hassle Trumps,' Red said.

'It's time they started,' I said. 'How about the girl? April Kyle? She one of yours?'

'You ain't a cop.'

'No.'

Red looked at Hawk. 'He ain't either,' he said. It wasn't a question.

I held April's picture up. It was a graduation picture with the hokey overripe color that school pictures always have. April was smiling. Her hair was long to her shoulders and brushed back like Farrah Fawcett. Styles die hard in the subs. The neck of a sweater showed in the picture and the frilly little round collar of her blouse. Behind the bar the first trio of nudes came back onto the runway. The air was hot and thick with smoke—some of it was pot.

'Yeah, I had her for a while,' he said. 'She split.'

'When?'

Red shrugged. 'Week ago, maybe—hard to

keep track, you know? I got a lot of girls.'

'Where's she live?'

'South End, Chandler Street.'

'What address?'

'Hell, man, I don't remember—she's got a room down there someplace.'

'You remember,' I said. 'You know where all your girls are. You probably got half a dozen girls in the same building.'

'No way, man, I don't do that. These kids come in here and they don't know their ass from a hole in the ground. They get in trouble. All I do is organize them a little. Look out for them on the street.'

'And they call you Uncle Red and giggle when you tickle them,' I said.

Red looked at his empty coffee cup. 'Hey, man,' he said in his soft voice. 'I'm telling you straight.'

I shook my head. 'I'm too old to listen to horseshit,' I said. 'Gimme the address and we'll be on our way.'

Red looked at Hawk beside him. Hawk smiled. Red looked back at me. 'I ain't scared of you,' he said. He jerked his head at Hawk. 'Him either.'

I said to Hawk, 'Where did we go wrong?'

Hawk was motionless with his hands folded on the table before him. When he had

67

no reason to move, his repose was nearly stonelike. His face had a perpetual look of noncommittal pleasure. Without changing his expression Hawk hit Red across the throat with his left hand. Red gasped and rocked back against the booth. He put both hands to his throat and made harsh wheezing noises. Hawk didn't look at him. He was back into repose, his hands quietly clasped in front of him.

'Soon as you can talk,' he said, 'tell Spenser the address.'

We sat quietly, listening to the harsh music. The crowd had thinned. The girls shuffled on the runway. The smoke drifted through the pink spotlight in ragged wisps. It was a hot and joyless room, nearly full of people, nearly devoid of humanity. Red was rocking back and forth, both hands clutching his throat. Twice he started to speak and nothing came out. Finally he said in a soft croak, 'Three Eighteen and a half. Three Eighteen and a half Chandler Street. Apartment Three B.'

I gave Red a card. 'If you run into April, get in touch with me,' I said.

He nodded, still holding his throat. His eyes were wet. Hawk and I got up.

'Shoulda been scared,' Hawk said.

CHAPTER TEN

The South End was a mix of winos and upscale young ad men in Gucci loafers. Some of the old red brick row houses had been sandblasted and festooned with hanging plants, so that they looked like the kind of restaurant where they serve carafe wine and quiche. Others had been left in their natural state and in them people slept four and five to the bed.

Three Eighteen and a half Chandler was not upscale. The door to the foyer was warped, so it wouldn't close. I pushed it open, and Hawk and I stepped into the foyer. It was empty except for a crumbled Nissen's bread wrapper and a long-dead starling. There were brass mailboxes along the left-hand wall. The fronts of all of them had been torn off and there was no mail in any of them. There were doorbell buttons with name tag slots beside them. All the slots were empty. The glass inner door had been broken and patched with plywood. Graffiti was spray painted all over the plywood in intricate curves.

Hawk pushed at the inner door. It swung

open. The doorjamb where the latch tongue fitted was torn away as if a strong person had kicked it in. We went in. The floor inside was small octagonal tiles that must have been white when they were put down but now seemed a brownish gray. Stairs went up the right wall.

Hawk said, 'I think I rather get laid in an MG.'

'It would be discouraging to have your date bring you here,' I said.

We started up the stairs. The walls were plaster that had been painted and repainted so that the surface was now lumpy and thick with the layers. The color was about the same as the floor. On the second-floor landing was an empty bottle. LIME FLAVOURED VODKA, the label said. There were three doors on the third floor. A ceiling fixture glared, shadeless, down on us.

There were no numbers on the doors. In the tiny hallway under the ugly light surrounded by blank doors I felt a little disengaged, remote from Susan, from open water, from baseball. I put my ear against the door nearest me. No sound. Hawk listened at the next door and I moved on to the third. Nothing.

'B should be the middle one,' I said,

'counting from either direction.'

Hawk nodded and rapped on the middle door. No one answered. He rapped again. No one. He tried the knob. The door didn't open.

'Gimme room,' I said. Hawk stepped out of the way. I kicked the door. And in we went. There were two people on a mattress on the floor. One was a young black woman, the other was a middle-aged white man with a roll around his middle. He was trying to scramble into his pants. He had them on and pulled up but not yet buttoned when we went in. The girl was naked and made no attempt to cover herself. She sat with her back against the wall, her legs out straight in front of her. She had the same look on her face that the dancers did in The Slipper. Nobody said anything. The man continued to struggle with his pants.

'Don't worry,' I said. 'This isn't trouble. We're looking for a young woman named April Kyle.'

'She ain't here,' the girl said.

'We were told she was,' I said. 'Apartment Three B.'

'This Three C,' the girl said.

'Elementary, my dear Holmes,' Hawk said.

I ignored him. 'Which is B? I said.

The man had his pants buckled and was working on his shoes. They were boots, actually—black, with a zipper on the side—and he struggled to ram his foot in from his half-sprawled position with obsessive intensity.

'Other end of the hall.'

'Do you know April Kyle?' I said.

She shook her head. The harsh light spilling in from the hall was nearly theatrical, making shadows under her cheekbones and breasts. I held out April's picture. 'How about her—ever see her?'

The girl didn't bother to look. She kept shaking her head.

'Take a look,' I said.

She kept shaking her head. Her dark eyes were empty. Her shoulders were hunched a little by the way she rested her hands, palm flat on the mattress. Her partner had one boot on and bent his every effort on the other one. His fat hairy upper body bent nearly double over his thighs as he struggled with the zipper.

I put the picture away. 'Would you like us to take you anywhere?' I said to the girl.

Same thing, slow headshakes right and left and right and left.

Hawk gestured at 3B with his head. I nodded. The man got his other boot zipped. I looked again at the girl sitting stock still. Her head still moved back and forth. I turned and went back in the hall. Hawk stepped out behind me.

'There's no logic to the numbering system,' I said.

'Why'd you think there would be?' Hawk said.

I knocked on 3B. All was quiet. I knocked again. Hawk said, 'My turn,' and I moved out of the way, and he kicked the door in. There was a bed in this room. A narrow metal bed painted white with a mattress on it and threadbare tufted chenille spread over the mattress. The bed was empty. So was the room. Besides the bed, the only thing in the room was a picture on the wall. It was a Polaroid color snapshot of a house. It looked familiar. It was April Kyle's house. In the hall behind us the man from 3C scooted down the stairs. The girl was standing in the open doorway watching us, left shoulder leaning against the doorjamb, hand on right hip. I looked around this room. There was a light switch beside the door. I turned it on. The overhead bulb was as unkind as the one in the hall. We stripped the spread back off the bare

73

mattress, looked under the mattress, under the bed, felt around the door molding. At the far end of the narrow room a dirty window faced onto an airshaft. I opened it and felt around within arm's reach in all directions.

'There's nothing here, babe,' Hawk said.

'I know.'

'You wanna try A?' he said.

'Good to be thorough,' I said. No one was in A. No girl. No man. No passion. No commerce. No ecstasy. No clues, either. It took five minutes to be certain of that. When we were through, all we had was the naked girl standing in the doorway of the empty room with the bare light dramatizing everything.

I looked at her. 'What are we going to do with her?' I said.

Hawk said, 'Nothing to do with her.'

I still looked at her.

'You looking to have a little fun?' she said.

'No,' I said. 'I'm not looking to have any fun at all.'

Hawk started down the stairs. 'C'mon, man, you keeping her from her work.'

I went after him. Down the narrow, filthy stairs. We checked the rest of the building. It was empty. On Chandler Street I said, 'I don't like that. There ought to be

74

something.'

We walked toward the car.

'Ought?' Hawk said. 'We both know what ought is worth.'

I nodded. 'How old you figure she is?' I said.

'Middle-aged, babe. She be dead when she's thirty.' His face under the streetlight as we got in the car was entirely without expression.

Hawk and I went back to The Slipper, but Red wasn't there, and he wasn't anyplace else, either, that we could discover. Trumps was gone too. I was beginning to feel like Winnie-the-Pooh. The more I looked for April Kyle, the more she wasn't there. It was eleven o'clock—my second night out in the Combat Zone. I had almost as much thrill as I could handle.

Outside a movie advertising an adult double feature with an all-male cast, Hawk said to me, 'This got a funny smell to you?'

'You mean how much trouble we're having finding one kid when we started out knowing where she was?'

'Yeah.'

'You think people don't want her found?'

'Yeah.'

'Maybe,' I said. 'Or maybe we just haven't

run across her.'

'We usually pretty good at running across things,' Hawk said.

'Yeah. Probably been distracted by the excitement of our surroundings,' I said.

Several men going into the theater eyed Hawk as they passed. No one spoke to him or to me.

'Make the blood just boil through your veins, don't it?' he said. 'All that glamour?'

'Yippee,' I said. 'I think I'll go home and brush my teeth. You want me to drop you someplace?'

Hawk shook his head. 'Just soon walk,' he said.

I nodded and started up Tremont.

'You keep an eye out for Trumps,' Hawk said. 'He hate to lose.'

'It's hard to get used to,' I said.

CHAPTER ELEVEN

I took a long hot shower before I went to bed, and drank three bottles of Rolling Rock extra pale, and ate a meatloaf sandwich on wheat bread from Rebecca's. My copy of *Sartoris* still lay on the bedside table at Susan's, so I

76

made do with a novel by John le Carré. And liked it. I fell asleep after one more beer and dreamed that Hawk and I were being chased by George Smiley, who looked just like Alec Guinness. I kept looking without success for Susan.

I woke up at ten past seven with the sun making the dust motes dance in the air. It was Saturday. Susan would be off. If I was prompt, we could have breakfast together.

No one was in front of the bowling alley as I drove toward Smithfield at ten of eight. Plenty of time for hanging out, good seats available all day. Life moved easy in Smithfield. In Boston women were already hooking in the Combat Zone.

When I got to Susan's she was up and wearing a blue warm-up suit with a white stripe down the leg. She gave me a kiss when I came in the kichen door.

'I was going to run,' she said. 'Want to come along? I'll slow down for you.'

The running stuff I kept at Susan's was somewhat more informal than hers: maroon sweat pants with a drawstring, a black wool turtleneck sweater, and a gray sweat shirt with the sleeves cut off to wear over the sweater. My gray New Balance running shoes had a lot of shoe glop patching.

'You look like you run for the Rescue Mission Track Club,' Susan said.

We jogged slowly along Main Street. Susan's pace was not a challenge. The temperature was in the forties. There was no wind. The sun splashed clean shadows on the road ahead of us. Nobody much was out in Smithfield at 8:15 on a Saturday.

'No luck on April,' Susan said.

'No.'

'Do you know if she is in fact a whore?'

'Yes. She's got a pimp named Red. I've talked with him. I talked with Amy Gurwitz. Hawk and I found a place on Chandler Street where she'd been. There was a picture of her house on the wall.'

'Her house?'

'Yeah. No Mommy and Daddy, no friends or siblings—just the house.'

We passed the junior high school, its lawn still green in November. Its circular drive empty of cars.

'That's very sad,' Susan said.

'Yes.'

'You've brought Hawk into this?'

'Yeah.'

'Is this a more complicated thing than it looked when you started?'

'Maybe,' I said. 'I aggravated a pimp, and I

78

figured I'd better have Hawk to watch my back. Also Hawk knows the guy that runs most of the street prostitution around there. Guy named Tony Marcus. I figured he'd be useful.'

'And you haven't found her, you and Hawk?'

I shook my head. Susan looped around the circular drive at the junior high school and headed back toward her house.

'This is going to be about two miles,' I said.

'Yes. That's what I always run.'

'You're doing the two hardest,' I said. 'The first and the last miles are always bad.'

'If I did more than two,' Susan said, 'I wouldn't do any.'

We'd had the conversation twenty times before. I nodded.

Susan said, 'Isn't it odd that you and Hawk together can't find her? I mean, if she's in the Combat Zone. It's not that big.'

'Yes. It's odd. We could keep missing her while she's plying her trade, but...' I shrugged.

Behind the small shopping center in the center the same barrel-bodied Lab I'd seen before was foraging in the dumpster near the market. The buildings around the Common were square and graceful, the sun emphasizing their whiteness, the unleaved trees black in filigreed contrast. We were quiet. As we turned down Susan's street I could smell wood smoke. Conservation chic.

'A shower will feel good,' Susan said as we walked in her driveway.

'I'd better stay with you,' I said. 'Never can tell who might be lurking in behind the shower curtain.'

'Golly,' Susan said. 'I feel so safe with you.'

I built a fire in the living room while Susan started the coffee. Then we showered. Susan's downstairs shower was very roomy with a sliding door and we were damned near hysterical with laughter in there before we got clean. I made a suggestion that Susan turned down.

'I'll drown,' she said.

Clean and wrapped in large towels but not quite dry, we went into the living room. The fire was hot and bright.

'I wouldn't drown in here,' Susan said.

'Couch or floor,' I said.

'The rug is thick.'

'Floor it is,' I said, and put my arms around her. Both towels slipped to the floor.

With her mouth against mine Susan said,

'No missionary position, big fella. The rug's not that soft.'

'Neither am I.'

'Elegant,' she murmured. 'Positively ritzy.'

CHAPTER TWELVE

Across the kitchen table Susan was wearing a white T-shirt that said on the front BALLOONS OVER BOSTON. Under the legend there were some multicolored balloons. She sipped coffee and watched me make breakfast.

'It's Spenser's famous corn cakes, this morning,' I said. 'We got any of that maple syrup we made last spring?'

'In the peanut butter jar in the refrigerator.'

I got it out and put it to warm in a saucepan. Then I measured equal parts of cornmeal and corn flour into a bowl.

'You're not happy with this April Kyle thing,' Susan said.

'No.' I put in some baking powder. 'No, I don't like the way we can't find her, and then we went back and looked for her pimp and we couldn't find him.'

'There's more,' Susan said. 'There's something else. You are not...' Susan thought a minute. 'You're a little inward.'

I beat two eggs and some milk together with a whisk.

'It's the scene,' I said. 'I am not new to misery, but it is the flat unalterability of it, I guess. You spend a couple days in the Combat Zone and you feel like you've eaten a bowl of grease.'

Susan nodded. 'It's not like you've never encountered depravity,' she said.

I added the milk and eggs to the flour and made a batter.

'I know, but it's depressing. Maybe there's a depravity tolerance and I've reached it. There was a black whore, maybe twenty-five, maybe thirty, and her pimp was going to beat her up for no good reason and I said I'd take her with me and she laughed.' I added a little corn oil to the batter. 'And she was right. Where in hell was I going to take her? Look in the yellow pages under C for convent?'

I oiled the griddle and turned the heat on under it.

'And there was a black kid about fifteen screwing some middle-aged white guy in a chemical suit on a bare mattress in an empty room. He took off when we showed up looking for April, and the kid wanted to know if I was interested.'

I put four small circles of batter on the hot griddle and watched them spread and begin to rise. When the bubbles began to show through I flipped them and after another minute I put two on Susan's plate and two on mine.

Susan put on butter and homemade maple syrup and took a bite. 'Yum,' she said.

'Only one yum?'

'I don't want you to get arrogant.'

I ate a pancake. 'Carbohydrate replenishment,' I said. 'After the exhausting run.'

'It wasn't the run that exhausted you,' Susan said.

'Maybe I should have scalloped some oysters.'

We ate two pancakes apiece and I put on four more.

'It makes you feel helpless,' Susan said.

'Yeah.'

'Hawk have any reaction?'

I shook my head. 'Far as I can tell, the world amuses the hell out of Hawk.'

'What fools these mortals be?'

I put two more corn cakes on each plate. 'Yeah,' I said, 'him and Puck.'

'Does the fact that so many of these women are black make you feel more of an outsider? More ... *naïve*'s not the right word, but somewhere in that area.'

'Possible,' I said. We ate. Susan poured me some more coffee. I put on another quartet of corn cakes. 'How many do you suppose we can eat before we hurt ourselves?'

'I can't speak for you,' Susan said. 'I'll stop with these two.'

'But mostly,' I said, 'it's spending time in a world where fifteen-year-old girls are a commodity, like electrified dildos, or color-coordinated merkins, and crotchless leather panties. It's a world devoted to appetite, and commerce.' I sipped some coffee. 'I think we are in rats' alley,' I said, 'where the dead men lost their bones.'

'Well,' Susan said, 'we are bleak about this. You want to stop?'

'No,' I said.

'I know you're doing this for me. I care more about you than about April Kyle. If you drop it, I'll understand.'

I shook my head.

'You can't,' she said.

'No.'

We were quiet. 'Maybe just two more,' I said.

84

Susan nodded. She looked at me with that power of concentration that she had. 'Why can't you?' she said.

I shrugged. 'It's what I do,' I said.

'Even when it bothers you like this?'

'If you only do it when it's easy, is it worth doing?'

She smiled. Her mouth was wide, and when she smiled her whole face smiled and her eyes gleamed.

'You never disappoint,' she said. 'You and Cotton Mather.'

I kept looking at her smile. It made up for a lot of things. Maybe it made up for everything.

'I'm not sure,' I said, 'that I could make it without you.'

'You could,' Susan said, 'but you'll never have to.'

CHAPTER THIRTEEN

I went back to work Sunday afternoon. At four o'clock I was having a drink with Hawk at J. J. Donovan's in the North Market.

'You want me to come along and keep you from getting mugged?' Hawk said. He had white wine. I had beer.

'No, I'll risk that alone,' I said. 'I want you to look into things from the other end.'

'Tony Marcus?'

'Yeah.'

'That's the top end.'

'True,' I said. 'You start there and I'll keep rooting around down here at the bottom. Maybe if I work up and you work down we'll meet somewhere and know something.'

'You care how I do it?' Hawk said. He sipped some wine.

'No. You know Marcus. You know the people around him. See if anything is up. All I want is the kid.'

Hawk nodded. He sipped some more wine. 'You going back and look around the Zone again.'

I nodded. My beer was gone. The bartender drew me another.

Hawk was looking at me. 'You know Marcus,' Hawk said.

'Yeah.'

'You know if something is up, it is something very heavy.'

'Yeah.'

'There be a lot of weight to take,' Hawk said. 'I don't mind. But you sure you ready?'

'What's bothering you, Hawk?' I said.

86

'This thing is queer,' he said. 'Since Friday I been asking around—a few pimps, a few hookers, some people I know. Everybody tight on this. Everybody don't know a thing. Everybody changes the subject. Everybody awful careful about some sixteen-year-old high school kid going home to her mommy.'

'See what you can get from Marcus,' I said. 'And try not to make him mad.'

Hawk smiled his antediluvian smile and left. I paid the bill and headed for the Zone.

It was jumping on a late Sunday afternoon, glowing like rotten wood. Somebody had said that about the English court once. Raleigh? I couldn't remember. I drifted south along Washington Street looking for a young white whore. I saw some, but they weren't April. Near Stuart Street I saw a white Jaguar sedan that might have been Trumps's. I felt the weight of my gun in its hip holster. A pleasing weight. Comforting. The jag pulled away from the curb and disappeared in the traffic. I saw the black whore with the crescent-shaped scar that I'd seen with Trumps my first night in the Zone. She was standing in front of a club that advertised ALL BOTTOMLESS on several cardboard signs in the window. She was wearing a white dress with a fluffy white fake fur collar. She spoke to a man walking past. He shook his head and walked faster. I stood beside her and said, 'How much for the night?'

She looked at me and opened her mouth and then closed it. 'I know you,' she said.

'To know me is to love me,' I said. 'How much?'

'No deal, mister. Just stay away from me.'

'Two bills,' I said. 'We'll go to my place.'

'Trumps would kill me,' she said.

'He doesn't need to know. I'm just across the Common. We'll spend a couple of hours and then you're back. He doesn't have to know. Two hundred bucks.'

She shrugged. 'Sure, why not,' she said.

We caught a cab at Boylston Street. It was maybe a ten-minute walk to my place, but she was wearing three-inch heels and could barely stand.

In my apartment she checked herself in the hall mirror and looked around.

'You want a drink?' I said.

'Gin and Seven-Up,' she said. I controlled a shudder.

'I don't have any Seven-Up,' I said. 'Gingerale?'

'Sure.'

I went into the kitchen to make her drink. When I came back she had taken off her dress. She had on scanty rayon underclothes. K mart erotica. 'You like to undress me or you want I should strip all the way?' she said.

'I just want to talk,' I said. 'I'm very lonely.'

She shrugged. 'Long as I get the bread,' she said. 'You gonna give me the bread?'

I handed her the gin and ginger ale, put my bottle of Rolling Rock extra pale on the coffee table, took out my wallet, and extracted two hundred-dollar bills. That left me $5, but I didn't let her see. I held them out. She took them, folded them over, and slipped them inside her underpants. Then she sat on the couch, put her feet on the coffee table, leaned back, and took about a third of her drink.

'Talk,' she said. 'Tell me about your life.'

There were bruises on her ribs.

'I'm interested in finding this kid, April Kyle,' I said.

She drank some more of her drink. He face was empty. 'That's nice,' she said.

'There'd be a good reward.'

'Uh-huh.'

'What harm if I find her? Who cares? Why not help me?'

Her drink was gone. I got up and made her another one. When I came back she was looking at the picture of Susan on the bookcase.

'Yours?' she said, and pointed her chin at the picture.

'Yes.'

'Married?'

'No.'

'That why you just wanna talk?'

'One reason.'

'What else, I don't turn you on?'

'Oh, yeah, you get my attention sitting around with your ass sticking out. It's just that I'm working, and I sort of need to concentrate on that.'

She nodded. 'And you don't like paying for it none either.'

'Not too much.'

'How you know somebody like Hawk?'

'We used to fight on some of the same cards a long time ago,' I said.

'Hawk ain't nobody to mess with,' she said.

'How do you know I know Hawk?'

She took a long swallow. 'I heard,' she said. 'I heard you was with him.'

'Trumps give you those bruises?'

'Uh-huh.' She finished the drink and held the glass out. 'This is an easy two hundred, honey.'

I brought the gin and ginger ale and ice out

on a tray and put them on the coffee table. I fixed her a fresh drink.

'Not too much ginger ale, honey. Don't want to spoil the gin.'

'So how come nobody wants me to find April?'

She smiled and drank and smiled again and shook her head.

'What's your name?' I said.

'Velma,' she said. 'Velma Fontaine.'

'Pleased to meet you, Velma. I'm Lance Cartaine.'

She squinted at me a little. 'Your name's Spenser.'

'Well maybe.'

'You jiving me?'

'Just a little, Velma. It's a bad habit of mine. I tend to jive almost everybody.'

She drank some more gin and ginger ale. She liked it. I thought it would gag a skunk, but I never had any skill with gin anyway.

'You jiving with the wrong people now,' Velma said.

'Like who?'

She smiled again. And shook her head again. I was beginning to think better of Trumps for whacking her.

'You know where the kid is?'

'Maybe.'

I drank another sip of Rolling Rock.

'You don't believe me?' Velma said. Her glass was empty. She leaned over and made herself another drink.

I shrugged.

'She ain't anyplace you'll find her.'

I didn't say anything. Susan says that's my best conversational ploy. Velma drank her drink. It was mostly gin, one ice cube, a splash of ginger.

'She been bad.'

I nodded.

'Stupid little bitch. She had it easy and she fucked it up. Then you come poking around and now she in real trouble.' More gin. 'She fixed up a nice house, nice call job, no street hooking, and she couldn't handle it. So Red gets her.'

I smiled slightly, encouraging, *Yes, yes, my dear, tell me all about it,* nondirective.

'You ain't gonna find her.'

'Probably not,' I said. Sad. Defeated. Winsome and childlike.

'You know why you ain't gonna find her?'

'No.'

Velma smiled again. ''Cause she ain't even in the city,' Velma said. 'You got any cigarettes?'

I shook my head.

'There's some in my dress, you want to get them for me, honey-Lance.' She laughed, a bubbly choked laugh, as if she had a bad cold. I got up and found a package of NOW menthol 100's in her pocket and a book of matches. I took out a cigarette and lit it and handed it to her. She'd better be drunk if she was going to go for that one. She was. She did.

'Hey, Lance. You got a lot of class, honey.'

The taste of the cigarette was still in my mouth. How the hell had I ever smoked them? They were as bad as gin and ginger ale.

Velma took a long drag on the cigarette, a big pull at her drink, swallowed, and let the smoke ooze out through her nostrils.

'Providence,' she said.

'Providence.'

She smoked some more, another long drag that made the end of the cigarette glow. 'You know what a sheep ranch is?'

'No.'

She was quiet. She smoked. She drank some gin. She refilled her glass and drank some more gin. She was older than I'd thought. Her thighs had thickened and there was a suggestion of dimpling to them. The line where the buttocks merged with her upper thigh had blurred. Her stomach folded a little as she sprawled on the couch.

'Sheep ranch for people like it kinky. You a whore and you bad, you end up there.'

'And April's at a sheep ranch in Providence?'

'I never said that,' Velma said.

'You know where there's a sheep ranch in Providence?'

'Never been there,' Velma said. 'Never been nowhere. Never been out of Boston.' Tears filled Velma's eyes and spilled over and traced down her face. Her voice thickened. 'Never been nowhere,' she said. 'Never going.' She sprawled lower onto my couch, her legs sprawled across my coffee table. She spilled her drink and didn't notice.

'There an address for the sheep ranch?' I said.

She didn't answer. She was crying and snuffling and mumbling things I couldn't understand. She slipped down farther and closed her eyes and stopped crying. She snuffled for another minute, then she was silent. Then she started to snore. I got up and went to the kitchen and got another bottle of beer and brought it back and sat down and stared at Velma while she slept.

It was two hours before she woke up, and when she did she was unfriendly. I got her dressed and into a cab and went back upstairs to drink beer and think about sheep ranches.

CHAPTER FOURTEEN

Providence is an hour south of Boston on Route 95. It has Brown University and the Rhode Island School of Design and a good-looking State House and a civic center and Federal Hill, a recycled Italian neighborhood with concrete arches at the entrance on Atwell Avenue.

I didn't go to Federal Hill this trip. I went to the Biltmore Plaza on the square by the railroad station and checked in.

'Where can a guy get a little action in this town?' I said to the bellhop when he showed me my room. I was wearing a white wash-and-wear shirt, red and white checked polyester jacket, and maroon double-knit flare-bottomed slacks with white loafers and a white belt. I had spent nearly $100 on the outfit at Zayre's. When I go undercover I spare no expense. I wore a maroon tie with many small white horse heads on it, loosened at the collar. I had a pinky ring with a zircon set in onyx, and I reeked of Brut.

'We have music in our lounge, sir.'

I folded a five and tucked it into his hand. 'Uh-huh,' I said. 'You don't follow my drift. I mean action, broads, huh?'

'Sorry, sir,' he said. 'I really wouldn't know about that.' He smiled and backed out and shut the door. I hung up my garment bag and went out to the front of the hotel and caught a cab.

'Ride down Dorrance,' I said. 'I want to look over the town.'

'Yes, sir,' the cabby said.

'I'm looking to have a little fun,' I said. I had another five folded between my fingers and I tapped it on the back of the seat as I leaned forward to talk with him. 'Anyplace in this town a guy can have a little fun?'

The cabby glanced back at me. 'What kind of fun, mister?'

'You know—wine, women, and song.' I grinned. Man to man. 'And I could do without the song, if I had to.'

The cabby was a middle-aged black man with short graying hair and a salt-and-pepper mustache. 'You looking for whores?'

'You got it, man. You got my message. Can you help me out?'

The cabby shook his head. 'I'm not a pimp,' he said. 'You got an address, I'll take

96

you there.'

'I was hoping you'd know.' I flourished the five a little.

'Nope.' He pulled over at a corner. 'Whyn't you try another cabby.'

I got out without saying anything and he drove off. I flagged another cab and we went through the routine again. I rode around Providence in a succession of cabs for about three hours with the worst collection of prudes I'd ever seen. It was twenty minutes to four when I finally scored. The cabby I scored with looked like a toad.

'I might be able to put you in touch with a guy,' he said. He was fat and short and he seemed to have settled seatwards from years of driving a hack. He didn't turn around as we drove along Fountain Street past the Providence police and fire headquarters. In Providence the cops wore brown uniforms and drove brown-and-white cruisers. I was pretty sure you could never solve a crime wearing a brown uniform. Maybe it was in honor of the university.

'Appreciate it,' I said. 'There's a sawbuck in it for you.' I had upped the ante after hour two.

'Cost you twenty dollars for me to put you in touch with this guy,' the cabby said. 'Plus the fare.'

'Just to meet a guy? Hey, that's pretty stiff.'

'Take it or leave it.' The cabby had a hoarse voice. The folds of his neck spilled over his collar.

'Aw, what the hell,' I said. 'It's only money, huh? You can't take it with you.'

The cabby put his hand back over the seat without looking. I put two tens in it. He tucked it into a shirt pocket, turned right, and in two minutes he pulled in at the curb on Dorrance Street in front of the Westminster Mall. Without looking back he said, 'That'll be three-eighty.' I gave him a five and he put that in a different pocket.

I said, 'How about my change.'

'Tip,' he said. Then he handed me back a plain white sheet of paper. 'Roll that up in your left hand and walk down the mall,' he said. 'Guy's name is Eddie. He'll find you.'

I took the paper, made a tube out of it, and got out of the cab. The toad pulled away. To my left was the flossiest Burger King in the world; ahead stretched a paved pedestrian way among a bunch of stores in the process of restoration. Some very classy fronts were mixed in with some very sleazy ones, but the place had the nice live feel that open city space has if a lot of people are bustling around in it.

I started up the mall. A squat red roan horse was tethered to an information booth in the middle of the mall and a Providence cop was in getting warm with the civilians. Near a soon-to-be-rented-but-not-fully-restored storefront a guy in a down vest said, 'How ya doing? I'm Eddie.'

I said, 'Hey, how are ya?'

He walked along beside me. 'What can I do for you?' he said.

'Fella in a cab told me you could find me a little action,' I said.

Eddie nodded. He had pale blond hair parted on the left and gold-rimmed glasses and pale skin. Under the down vest he wore a plaid shirt. 'Sure,' he said. 'What kind of action you looking for?'

'Well'—I scowled and looked embarrassed—'I hear you might have something different around here.'

Eddie stopped with his hands in his back pockets and looked at me. 'Unusual?'

I spread my hands, 'Yeah, a little kinky, you know. Sometimes you like a change.'

'What kinda bread you ready to pay?'

'Oh, I got money. Listen, that's not a problem. I can pay.'

Eddie nodded again. Then he nodded and winked. 'Yeah, I can fix you up. Cost you two bills—one to me, one to the manager of the place. You got that?'

'Sure.'

'After that it depends what you want, you understand. You want more than one broad, that's extra, you want S and M, that's extra. Get the idea?'

I nodded.

'And you want to tip any of the broads, that's between you and them.'

I nodded.

'Gimme two hundred,' he said. 'I'll drive you up.'

I took a hundred and five twenties from my wallet and gave them to Eddie. He counted them and put them away and led me down a narrow cross street to a Pontiac Firebird Trans Am. We got in and headed up the hill toward the university. We went past the School of Design and Brown University, past some of the most elegant Victorian houses anywhere. In ten minutes Eddie parked the Trans Am on Angel Street near the corner of Stimson, in front of a deep blue three-storied Victorian house with a vast mansard roof. Over the windows was an ornamental sunrise design in yellow and black.

'This is it,' he said, and got out of the car. I followed him. We went up three wide wooden stairs and across a deep veranda and Eddie rang the doorbell. A husky young man wearing a green Lacoste sweater over a white shirt opened the door. He had a health club tan, a bushy mustache and dark hair blown dry.

Eddie said, 'Fella to see Mrs. Ross.'

The man nodded. Eddie gave him my hundred-dollar bill. The man smiled at me and said, 'This way, sir.'

He showed me into a high-ceilinged living room with a marble fireplace and bow windows on two walls. I sat on a hard sofa with claw-and-ball feet, and the man went away. In maybe a minute a woman came in. She was a small woman, middle-aged, with her gray hair in a frizzy perm. She wore a black turtleneck sweater and a pleated red plaid skirt and black boots. There was a gold medallion on a chain, and large hoop earrings, and rings on most of her fingers. She came in and stood in front of me. She had no makeup except for some red color on her cheeks that stood out against her white skin.

'Good afternoon,' she said. 'I'm Mrs. Ross. We have ten girls here. What kind of arrangement would you like to make?'

'I heard your girls do speciality stuff.'

'Anything you want,' she said firmly.

'All of them?'

'Absolutely.'

'Maybe I better meet them,' I said.

'Of course,' she said. 'Two are busy at the moment, but I'll ask the rest to come in and say hello. Would you care for a drink?'

I shook my head. 'Not right now.'

Mrs. Ross added. 'Certainly. I'll get the girls.'

She went back out and down the corridor and I sat quietly in the nineteenth-century room. Students on bicycles went by on Angell Street outside. I heard Mrs Ross's boot heels tapping briskly along the hardwood floor of the corridor, and then she came through the archway. Behind her came eight young women. Four were white, three were black and one was Oriental. The third one through the door was April Kyle.

The eight girls stood in an informal semicircle, staring blankly into the middle distance the way models do at a fashion show. They had each their own expression, and it didn't change. It was their stage face, I realized. The oldest was maybe nineteen, the youngest fourteen or fifteen. They were all dressed young, too, with a kind of buttons-

and-bows little-girl look that must have been calculated. April, for instance, was wearing a white blouse under a green plaid jumper with black knee socks and penny loafers. Her blond hair was caught back on one side with a barrette. The fun-loving Bobbsey.

'Your choice?' Mrs. Ross was not a dawdler, nor did she encourage it in others. I wondered if I ought to check their teeth.

'That one,' I said.

'Fine,' Mrs. Ross said. 'April, show the gentleman to your room.'

The other seven girls went out of the living room and April stepped toward me, put out her hand, and said, 'My name's April, what's yours?'

'Alley Oop,' I said.

She smiled without warmth or meaning. 'Okay, Alley, want to come with me?'

'Hey,' I said with a big hearty smile, 'I'd follow you anywhere, honey.'

She took my hand. In the hallway there was a wide stairway that turned halfway up. We went up the stairs hand in hand—*with wand'ring steps and slow*, I thought—turned at the landing, and continued to the big second-floor hallway. There were no rugs on the floor and no furniture. It was as if by the time you got here you were sold, and they didn't need to impress you. April's room was at the end of the hall on the right. We went in.

CHAPTER FIFTEEN

The room was Spartan. There was a good mahogany double bed and bureau. The window in the wall opposite the bed was covered with red drapes. Behind the entry door was a door that I assume led to a closet. April sat on the bed, letting her legs fall carelessly open. Unless she had a lot of self-control, she'd be fat when she was forty. Right now she was pretty in a pink-cheeked, almost plump way. Her mouth was pouty and her teeth were white and even. There was something theatrical about her movements when they occasionally became unrestrained, as when she had flopped on the bed.

I opened the door that I took to be a closet. It was. There were a few dresses hanging in it. There were also various leather restraints hanging from hooks and a wooden paddle that was too long for Ping-Pong and too short for canoeing. On the floor were a pair of sneakers and a pair of sling-back spike-heeled pumps—apparently she had more than one image. There was nothing else in the closet.

I turned back toward April. She had hiked the jumper skirt up over her thighs so that I was aware that she wore nothing beneath it. She looked at me with her stage look—pouty innocence, Lolita, Debbie Does Dallas. Probably practiced her look in the mirror between tricks.

I parted the drapes on the window. Under the drapes the window was secured with thick wire mesh. I let the drapes drop back in place. I looked over the rest of the room. There was no other way out. I didn't see any signs of a bug, though that didn't mean there wasn't one. On the top of the mahogany dresser was a radio. I turned it on. Loud.

On the bed April was naked except for her knee socks. There were dark bruises on her buttocks that had begun to yellow, her wrists were chafed red. I remembered the time when a girl her age would have excited me. But it was a long time ago—when I was her age. Now it was like looking at a naked child.

I lay down on the bed beside her and put my arm around her and held her close against me and whispered, 'My name is not Alley Oop, it's Spenser, and your parents hired me to find you.' Her body went rigid and she

105

tried to pull away. I held her against me. I said, 'You won't have to do anything you don't want to do. But if you want out of here, I'll take you out.'

April was perfectly rigid and silent. I had my mouth against her ear. 'I don't know if there's a bug in here, but there could be, so we'll whisper and leave the radio up loud.'

'A bug?'

'A microphone for listening to us,' I whispered.

'I don't know.'

'Now, you want out of here?'

She was silent.

'I think you do,' I said. 'It couldn't have been fun getting those bruises on your backside.'

'Don't you want to fuck me?' she said.

'Nothing personal, but no, I don't. I want to take you out of here and buy you dinner someplace and see what our next step is.'

She was still.

'Get dressed,' I said, my mouth still against her ear, my arms around her, holding her against me.

'They won't let me go,' she said.

'I'll take care of that,' I said. I let her go and sat up on the edge of the bed.

'Angelo,' she said, still whispering.

'That the disco prince downstairs?'

'Yes.'

'He the bouncer?'

'Yes,' she said. 'He has a gun.'

'But is he pure of heart?' I said.

She had slipped her blouse on. She stopped, half dressed. 'They won't let me.'

'Any other bouncers?' I said.

'During the day just Angelo. He gets off at seven and Monte and Dave come on for the night.'

I looked at my watch. Five past five. 'Good,' I said, 'we got them outnumbered.'

She had her jumper on now, and her knee socks. She slipped her feet into the penny loafers. 'What are you going to do with me after?'

'Buy you dinner, maybe some underwear. First we'll depart.'

'Angelo's got a gun,' she said again. Always she spoke in a whisper and never did she sound like anything much mattered. Angelo and his gun were a source of anxiety, maybe. But not much.

'I got one too,' I said. 'Let's go.'

We went out her door and down the corridor to the stairs. We were on the landing where they turned when Angelo appeared at the foot. Mrs. Ross was with him. April stopped.

'Come on, babe,' I said. 'Nobody with blow-dried hair ever gave me trouble.' We went down.

At the foot of the stairs Mrs. Ross said, 'Through so quickly, sir?'

Angelo stood in front of the door, looking at me carefully. He was obviously a body builder and he was big, but I was bothering him a little. He frowned.

'Ms. Kyle and I are going to dinner,' I said. 'You know—wine, candles, a little romance. Things are too commercial nowadays, I say.'

'I'm sorry,' Mrs. Ross said briskly, 'the girls are not allowed to date customers. April, go upstairs.'

April took a half-step back and I put my hand behind me and stopped her.

'Let's not dick around here,' I said. 'April's coming out with me, and Angelo isn't good enough to stop us.'

I hadn't bothered Angelo enough. He underestimated me. He put his left hand flat against my chest and shoved, the way he would have some guy in town for a convention. I took his wrist in my left hand and yanked his arm straight out across my body. I put my right hand against his elbow and levered him sprawling against the stairs. I kept hold of his wrist as he fell and turned his arm up behind him. Then I got hold of his hair with my right hand and dragged him back up to his feet and held him with his arm bent up and his head pulled back.

'Open the door, April,' I said.

'No,' Mrs. Ross said, and April froze.

I took a deep breath. 'Always the hard way,' I said. I shoved Angelo away from me and into Mrs. Ross. They both went down, Mrs. Ross backward, Angelo on top of her. By the time they got straightened out, I had my gun pointing at them and the door open for April.

Angelo's breath was rasping in and out.

Mrs. Ross said, 'You dumb cocksucker, you've gotten yourself in really big trouble. You don't know who owns this place, but you'll find out.' Her voice was hissing as she spoke.

I gestured at the door with my head. 'Come on, babe, let's go.'

April didn't look at Mrs. Ross. She walked straight out the door without looking at anything.

I said, 'If anybody sticks a nose out this door, I will put a bullet into his or her sinuses.'

Mrs. Ross was working on her theme. 'Dumb mother-fucker,' she hissed.

I backed out, closed the door, took April by the arm, and dragging her with me, ran like hell up Angell Street.

CHAPTER SIXTEEN

It took about a half hour for us to walk back to the Biltmore Plaza. It was cold and April had no coat. We couldn't find a cab, so I had to give her my jacket. That left the .38 in its hip holster out in the open air and several people looked at me askance as we went by. When we got to the lobby I retrieved my coat and covered the gun.

It took me a half hour to pack, check out, get my car, and head for home. In that time April had said not a word, but she stuck close to me. When we were heading up Route 95, I said 'Dinner in Boston, okay?'

'Okay.'

'Ever been to the Warren Tavern?'

'No.'

'It's in Charlestown, good place. Old. Food's good.'

She didn't say anything. I wasn't too

worried about Mrs. Ross and the friendly folks who owned the sheep ranch. It was probably connected, and Angelo was probably a mob watchdog. But they didn't know who I was, and they probably had a good supply of teenage whores. I checked the rearview mirror occasionally, but no one had followed us, and no one was following now.

'You going to take me home?' Her voice was louder than it had been in her room but not more animated.

'If you want me to.'

'What if I don't?'

'I won't.'

'They hired you to make me come home.'

'Actually, to find you.'

'You'll make me go home.'

'Nope.'

'I won't stay.'

It was dark now. We crossed the state line into Massachusetts at Attleboro.

'That bad at home?' I said.

She was quiet.

'Worse than the sheep ranch?'

Out of the corner of my eye I could see her shrug.

'How'd you get those chafe marks on your wrists?' I said.

'Lots of guys like to tie you up when they

do it,' she said in her small monotone.

'And the bruises on your butt?'

'Some guys like to paddle you.'

Route 95 had a wide dividing strip. The cars heading south were barely noticeable and not many cars were heading north. There was just the two of us in the small car, talking in the dark.

'And home's worse than that?'

'When you're not working, they leave you alone.'

'Except you couldn't leave,' I said.

'They left you alone. And . . .' Her voice stopped.

'You like the life?'

'Sure. Nobody hassles you. Nobody tells you what to do.'

'Except occasionally some stranger ties you up and hits you with a stick.'

'Yeah. They do other stuff too.'

'I imagine,' I said.

'You want to hear about it?'

'If you want to tell me.'

She shrugged again. 'Some guys like to hear about it.'

'I'm not one of them,' I said. 'If you want to talk about it, I don't mind hearing.'

She shook her head. I was watching the road and looking at her in quick peeks. She was slumped still in the seat of the MG. Her feet were out straight in front of her.

'How'd you end up in Providence?' I said.

'Red sent me down here.'

'Why?'

She shrugged again. It was a hard conversation to follow if you were driving.

'How'd you meet Red?' I said.

'You a cop?'

'No.'

'How come you had a gun?'

'Private cop,' I said.

'Umph.'

'Everybody is thrilled like that,' I said. 'How'd you meet Red?'

She shook her head.

'Red had you on the street before?'

'Uh-huh.'

'That's a tough work. Classy girl like you, I would think he might set you up in a call operation.'

She didn't comment.

'Weren't you a call girl first?'

'Yeah.'

'So how come you got demoted?'

'Red ordered me around too much. I don't like being ordered around.'

'So you were on the street and then Red sent you down here?'

'Yeah.'

'You getting punished again?' I said.

'No. I didn't give him any trouble. He just drove me down to Providence and said I had to work there.'

'When?'

'Last week?'

'When last week?'

She made an impatient gesture with her head. 'I don't know, last week sometime.'

'Today is Monday,' I said. 'How many days ago did you arrive?'

She was looking down at her knees, her feet pushed out straight in the low leg well of the sports car. It was dark, but I could see a sulky set to her shoulders.

'Come on, April, how many days?'

She shook her head in disgust and took a long exasperated breath and made a considerable show of thinking and counting on her fingers. She was overacting badly—I was already willing to believe that thinking came hard for her. 'Five days,' she said.

'Thursday,' I said.

'I guess so.'

'What time of day?'

'Jesus, mister, what difference does it make? Get off my ass, will you?'

'What time?'

'I don't know, late in the day.'

'Was it dark yet?'

'It was just getting dark.'

'Red put on the headlights?'

'Not at first.'

'Four maybe,' I said. 'Four thirty?'

'Sure,' she said.

'And you weren't having any trouble with Red?'

'No. When I started I got a little out of line maybe, and Red slapped me around and said I'd have to work the Zone for a month.'

'How long did you have to go?'

'Two weeks.'

'And you weren't getting out of line?'

'No.'

'So why'd he send you to the sheep ranch?'

'I don't know.'

'Isn't it usually a place they send troublemakers?'

She nodded.

'You a troublemaker?'

'Just that one time, honest to God. I only did it that one time.'

'What did you do?'

'I got a call and I didn't go. You know? I said I was going, and I went out and everything, but I didn't go. I went to the show instead. And Red finds out and he's pissed, right? And he beats the shit out of me and makes me work the Zone. But I was good after that. I didn't do a goddamned thing. I wanted to get back on call, you know? Guys take you to nice hotel rooms. You can sleep over, in-room movies sometimes, breakfast in bed, take a shower, everything, right? I wanted to get back on that. So I didn't give anybody any trouble.'

'Everybody's gotta have a dream,' I said.

'Just that one time,' she said. 'Only time I ever did anything bad.'

We were quiet then. She dreaming heavily of in-room movies and room service, me thinking about how she seemed to have been shipped to Providence shortly after I talked to Amy Gurwitz, before I spoke first with Trumps, and long before Red told me the Chandler Street address.

April said, 'Can you pull over a minute? I gotta go to the bathroom.'

'Want me to pull off at the next exit and find a gas station?'

'No, I gotta go real bad. Just stop here and I'll go in the woods. Please, I gotta go bad.'

I pulled over onto the shoulder and April got out as soon as the car stopped moving. She ran down the small gully along the road and up the other side and into the dark trees.

It took me maybe ten minutes to realize I'd been had. I waited another ten and got out and walked into the woods and yelled. Beyond the reach of the headlights on Route 95 the woods were opaque. I couldn't see anything, and I was pretty sure that by now there was nothing to see.

CHAPTER SEVENTEEN

I'm not a man who quits easily. I had planned on the Warren Tavern and, goddamn it, I went to the Warren Tavern. Susan went with me.

'The old pee-in-the-bushes trick,' Susan said, her eyes bright, 'and you fell for it.'

'The price of chivalry,' I said.

Susan sipped some white wine. 'At least we know her situation.'

'We did,' I said. 'And we can speculate that her new situation won't be a big improvement.'

Susan nodded. She was wearing a violet-colored knit dress and diamond earrings. Her dark hair was shiny, and she smelled of expensive perfume. I hadn't seen her since Saturday and it seemed a year. The waiter brought duck for me and scrod for her. The duck had a pecan stuffing beneath it. 'Rolling Rock, a duck, and thou,' I said, 'under the timbered roof.'

'Poetry,' Susan said. 'Everything you say is poetry.'

'And in action?'

'Epic,' she said. 'What are we going to do about April?'

'We can remember April and be glad,' I said. 'She doesn't want to come home.'

'She told you that?'

'Yes. She was happy to get out of the sheep ranch in Providence, but she wanted nothing to do with me.'

'Do you have a thought on where she'll go or what she'll do now?'

'Red, maybe. Her job skills are limited and she's gotta eat.'

Susan nodded, thinking. I spent a lot of time trying to decide whether she was more spectacular when she was serious or when she laughed. The energy level didn't change and in both cases the charge of her presence made breathing harder. I had never decided and maybe I wouldn't. The fun was in thinking about it.

'She'll be back in some kind of setting like that, I imagine,' Susan said. 'The forces that made her become a whore probably haven't changed. The things she hated about her home and her school and her town and herself presumably remain, whether or not she spent time in a—what do they call it?'

'Sheep ranch,' I said. 'You know—because it's kinky.'

Susan ate some scrod. 'In a way it must be a kind of perverse belonging.'

'To what?' I said.

'To the pimp, to the other girls who are no better than you, to'—Susan had her fingers cathedraled and tapped her upper lip—'to a world where she's desirable enough for people to pay.'

'A way to be valuable?'

'Yes,' Susan said, and smiled. When she smiled I always expected people to turn and stare. 'You're quite intuitive for a man with a seventeen-inch neck. It's a way to be valuable, even if only as a commodity, a product.'

I washed down a bit of pecan stuffing with a swallow of Rolling Rock. The bottle was empty. I gestured at the waitress and she went for more. Susan's glass was still half full. It was one of her few serious flaws.

'She's valuable to the customer,' Susan said, 'because he's willing to pay for her, if but briefly. She's valuable to the pimp in that she generates income, she's rental property.'

The waitress brought my beer. I drank some.

'And—I'm right, am I not?—the pimp takes care of her. Sees that she's paid, gets a bail bondsman if she's arrested, sees that she's not maltreated by the customer—at least, to the extent that she can't generate income?'

'Yes.'

'All of this is, of course, dehumanizing,' Susan said. She wasn't eating or drinking. She was single-mindedly following the trail of her speculation. She was explaining to me, but she was also explaining to herself. Thinking out loud. As I often did with her. She had very little peripheral vision. But I had never known anyone who could concentrate the way she could, once something got her attention. 'But perhaps being dehumanized is a kind of sedative for someone full of self-hate. It's a way of desensitizing yourself, and of course, your every experience tells you that the rest of the world is pretty lousy too.'

'Which makes you not so bad,' I said.

'So maybe she's better off.'

'Turning tricks instead of cheering for

Smithfield High? Better not spread that around the guidance office. Wasn't it Smithfield where heretics were burned?'

Susan smiled. 'That was Smithfield, England, I believe.'

'You suggesting I stop looking for her?'

'I suppose I can't say that. I suppose her parents should decide.'

I shook my head. 'I'm not doing it for the parents.'

'I know. And we both know the parents. Kyle will say he doesn't want her darkening his door, and Mrs. Kyle will cry and want her back.'

I nodded.

'What do you think?' Susan said.

'I think a couple of things,' I said, 'maybe several.' The waitress brought dessert menus. 'I think there's no point finding her and dragging her home because she'll just split again, and as far as I can tell, I don't blame her. I won't make her go home.'

'Indian pudding,' she said to the waitress, 'with vanilla ice cream. And black coffee.'

The waitress looked at me. 'Same,' I said. She smiled and went away.

'However,' I said to Susan, 'I don't think her life is all that good for her whoring. She may feel better about herself than she would at home being June Allyson, but there's not much there, either. She could get killed or onto smack or graduate to something worse than the sheep ranch'—I drank the rest of my beer—'and,' I said, 'there's something funny going on. They shipped her down to Providence almost the minute I started looking for her. I talked with Amy Gurwitz one afternoon, and April was off to the ranch before supper. They didn't want her found.'

'You mean Amy Gurwitz is involved?'

'Must be. Or someone in Smithfield. She was on the road before I ever started talking to management.'

Dessert arrived.

'All of which means what?' Susan said.

'Hell, I don't know. I can barely keep track of the news, let alone analyze it. But I think we better locate April again and see how she is, and while we're doing that maybe we can figure out what to do with her if she isn't swell.'

Susan was smiling. 'Also,' she said, 'you can't stand to have lost her, and you won't quit on this until you find her again.'

I swallowed some pudding. 'I'm a very neat person,' I said. 'I never leave an unmade bed. Want to go back to my place for a nightcap and a bit of free love?'

'We might get your bedclothes all wrinkled,' Susan said over her coffee cup.

I sighed. 'I know,' I said. 'I thought of that, but life is a trade-off. It'll be worth it.'

Susan finished her coffee and put her cup down and leaned a little toward me. Her dark eyes were enormous. 'You better believe it,' she said.

CHAPTER EIGHTEEN

Hawk was drinking white wine and soda at the bar in Gallagher when I came in. He had on a dark gray three-piece suit with a fine pinstripe, white shirt, pink collar, pink silk tie, and pink pocket hankie. There were diamonds winking in his gold cuff links and another glimmering in his right earlobe. His head gleamed in the bar's soft light as if he'd oiled it. I'd felt pretty good about my leather trench coat until I saw him.

'You stop somewhere and get your head buffed?' I said.

He made room for me at the bar. 'That's a halo,' he said.

I ordered beer. 'You know something or are you just lonely and I'm the only one can stand you?'

'Tony Marcus says they going to put you in the ground if you don't stop messing with his whores,' Hawk said. He drank some wine and soda.

I raised my eyebrows. 'So she is his,' I said.

'They all his, babe,' Hawk said.

'So why does he care about one more or less?' I said.

'He didn't say. He just said tell you that you going in the ground unless you back away.'

'He told you that himself?'

'Uh-huh.' Hawk grinned. 'I was visiting with him, being slick, seeing if I couldn't acquire a little intelligence without letting on, you know. And he say, "You still tight with Spenser?"—well, actually he say, "You still tight with that honky muthafucker?" but I knew who he meant, and I say, "Yeah," and he say, "You tell him stay away from my whores or he going in the ground."'

'Man's a racist,' I said.

'No doubt,' Hawk said, 'but he got enough people to do it.'

'I know,' I said. 'Why do you suppose it matters to him. What's special about this kid?'

Hawk shrugged. 'You making any

progress finding her?'

'I found her and lost her.'

Hawk smiled with pleasure. 'Lost her? Hell, I figured you was overmatched. How old is she?'

'Sixteen.'

'She didn't take your gun away, did she?'

'Hell, no,' I said. 'I'm no amateur.'

'What you going to do now?'

'I'm going to look for her some more. How about you? You still working for me or did Tony Marcus hire you away?'

'Always happy,' Hawk said, 'to take your money, long as you still alive.'

'Okay, pick up Red and stay with him. See if she surfaces there. If she does, bring her to me.'

'What if Red don't like it?'

'Reason with him.'

Hawk nodded. 'You sure it wouldn't be better for me to stick with you? Marcus wasn't jiving.'

'No. I'm going over and sit in the Back Bay and watch a house and see what goes in and out.'

'Okay.' Hawk finished the wine and left a five on the bar. 'You get aced, Susan gonna be awful mad,' he said.

'At both of us,' I said. 'You paying for

mine too?'

'Sure. It'll go on my bill.'

We got up and moved through the lunch hour crowd and out to the street.

Hawk headed up State Street to Washington and I went to get my car.

I drove round and round the block until I found a parking space on Beacon from which I could see Amy Gurwitz's house. Hawk could cover the Zone better than I could, especially since April would recognize me and not him, and the other option was watching this house. It wasn't much of an option, but it was better than driving around looking in windows, which was the only other thing I could think of.

Amy and April had been friends—or so they said at the bowling alley in Smithfield—on the run, with no money—hell, no coat. April might end up there. It was sunny and clear, not too cold for November, and the sun on the canvas roof of the MG had a greenhouse effect that made it comfortable without the heater. I tilted the seat back and stretched my legs out and stared at the Gurwitz front door for the rest of the afternoon. Nobody came out. Nobody went in. No one looked out a window. No smoke signals emanated from the chimney. No sound of demented laughter echoed from its corridors.

The streetlights went on, and lights in the windows up and down Beacon Street. At about 5:15 the front porch light went on at Amy's. At a little after six the same fat guy I'd seen before came trundling down Fairfield from the same alley as before and went up the steps and let himself in. He had on a plaid overcoat that looked like the saddle blanket for a hippopotamus. Then the light went out on the front porch and that was it. I hung on until nearly eleven at night and then went home and ate a baked bean sandwich on whole wheat with mayonnaise and lettuce and went to bed.

I was back on the job on Beacon Street before eight the next morning. It was the day before Thanksgiving and the street was busy with college kids going home for the holiday. I was prepared for a long siege today. I had some caponata from Rebecca's and some feta cheese and black olives and Syrian bread. I also had a large Thermos of coffee and a portable radio. I ate and listened to jazz and drank coffee and watched the coeds in their designer jeans and thought about what Susan and I would do for Thanksgiving dinner, and the day wore on.

I was listening to Ron Della Chiesa on WGBH. He was playing an album by Anita Ellis when the fat man came his usual route and went into the house. Early. I looked at my watch. 3:20. Out of work early for the holiday. I was listening to Teddi King with Dave McKenna's thumping piano behind her, when Fatso came out of the house with Amy and two suitcases. Off to Grandma's for a turkey dinner? Off to a country inn for roast goose with plum sauce? They went around the corner, up Fairfield Street, down the alley, and in maybe two minutes came driving out in a Volvo station wagon that fit the fat guy like a tailored shirt. They headed up Beacon while I decided what to do. By the time they'd reached the corner of Gloucester I knew what I'd do. I'd sit here for a while and if they didn't come back I'd burglarize their home and see what was what.

CHAPTER NINETEEN

Carol Sloan was just beginning to sing when I regretfully snapped off the radio and climbed out of the MG. I got a Speedo gym bag out of the trunk and went up Fairfield and down the alley behind the buildings and counted until I was behind Amy's. There was a small yard with a cast-iron fence around it, a gate that closed off a parking space, three green plastic trash barrels with lids, and beyond the little yard the French doors that I'd seen from the inside.

I stepped over the low fence and went to the French doors. They were locked. I knocked on the door and then smiled and waved through the glass at the empty living room. That was for anyone watching. Then I made a gesture at the doors, nodded, and set down my bag. I took a thin chisel and hammer out of it and began, quite carefully, to chip away the glazing compound around the frame of one pane in the French doors. The pane next to the latch. The process took maybe half an hour. The putty was old and dried hard. When I had it cleaned away, I put the hammer and chisel back in the bag and got out some long-nosed pliers and a screwdriver with a thin head and pried out the little V-shaped wedges they use to hold the glass in place under the putty. I got them out without bending them badly and put them in the bag. Then I took out a roll of adhesive tape, tore off a length, pressed about half of the length against the loosened pane, used the other half for a handle, and prying carefully with my screwdriver, I took the pane out without breaking it. I put it down out of the way and reached in through the opening and unlatched the French doors. With the door ajar I put the pane back into the frame, tapped the glaziers' wedges back into place, got out a can of glaziers' putty, and reputtied the pane into place. When I was done, you'd have to be very alert to notice it had happened. Then I put my tools back in the bag and picked up the bag and went into the living room and shut the door behind me and relocked it.

The house was as neat as I remembered. I took off my coat and laid it over a chair and walked through once to make sure it was empty. Walking quietly, listening hard, my gun offering a reassuring weight in my right hip pocket. I'd probably burgled a hundred homes in my life, but it was always the same, the tense feeling of intrusion. Uncertain, concentrated, full of tiny building sounds that you only heard when you were breaking and entering. And always in part listening for the distant siren getting louder. There was no one home.

Back in the living room I started to search. I took my time, one room at a time. If you don't want it known that you've searched a place it takes a lot longer. But I had time and I saw no reason to let anyone know I was still interested in Amy—or April. What Tony Marcus didn't know wouldn't hurt me.

The place looked like the world according to Bloomingdale's—wineglasses and bread baskets and copper cookware, Irish linen and English china and Scotch whisky and cookbooks by Julia Child, lacquerware and unglazed earthenware and brass umbrella stand and silver champagne buckets and crystal chandeliers and a wine rack full of French wines and chopping block counters and delft tile bathrooms.

On the second floor was an office with a rolltop desk and big black leather executive chair and a dictating machine and an IBM Selectric typewriter. On a coffee table was a briefcase in black leather that said MITCHELL POITRAS in gold embossing on the top. I opened it. It was full of correspondence on stationery headed Commonwealth of Massachusetts, Department of Education. The letters were full of gobbledygook about Chapter 762 and Title IX and programs impacting student populations, and people developing the pedagogical strategies, and a lot of stuff much less exciting than that. Most of them were addresssed to Poitras. His title was Executive Coordinator, Student Guidance and Counseling Administration. I felt humble. The desk was full of more of the same, including a lot of Core Evaluation forms, some of which seemed to have been coded in different-colored inks. There were also bills and a checkbook that indicated a balance of $23,000. Not bad for a state worker. Neither was the house. In the middle drawer there was a set of spare keys on a key ring. I pocketed them.

The master bedroom was pink silk, velvet, and satin with an enormous canopied bed. The other furniture was white and gold. The place looked like one of those bedrooms in the Pocono Mountain resorts with names like Honeymoon Haven and Wedding Night Manor—all it lacked was a heart-shaped bathtub. In the bottom drawer of the bureau was a matched set of vibrators. I was getting embarrassed. There was also a batch of nude pictures of Amy Gurwitz. She looked like a contestant in a Brooke Shields look-alike contest. High voltage.

I felt something like relief when I got out of the bedroom and up to the third floor. Maybe there'd be something to cleanse the palate up here—a woodworking set, or a model train collection. When I went in it looked encouraging. It seemed a photo setup. But it wasn't encouraging, it was a place for taking and processing dirty pictures. For an hour and a half I waded through a variety of glossy photos, video-tapes, and 8-millimeter reels. The room had it all—video-tape camera and recorder, movie camera, an old Rolleiflex on a tripod for still work, and files upon files of the product.

There is a limit to human invention, and pornographers seem to reach it early, but besides the sameness of pornography this collection had a special unifying theme. All the actors were young—high school age or less—both genders, and aimed at all sexual preferences. 'Ah, sweet bird of youth,' I said out loud. I was trying to work back up to embarrassment. My voice in the empty house was hoarse. Obviously some of the scenes had been shot in this town house. Some on the ornate canopied bed downstairs. Some in the living room where Amy had so properly served me a glass of beer on a walnut tray. Some you couldn't tell. I looked at all the snapshots to see if April was in any of them. She wasn't. I sampled a couple of tapes and a couple of films and didn't see her. It would have taken a week to go through the tapes and films.

I put everything back and went out and down the stairs. There was nothing more to do there. I went back and checked the French doors to be sure they were latched. Then I put my coat on and went out the front door, which locked behind me. I took the spare keys to a Sears store and had copies made. Then I went back to Poitras's place, unlocked his front door with my duplicate, returned his spares to the middle drawer, and left.

It was dark. I'd been in there for maybe six hours and it felt as if I'd been gone for the winter. I got in the MG and started it up and let the motor idle while I thought. In the dark November night the car was cold. When the engine warmed up I put the heater fan on. One of the things I thought about was the fact that Poitras seemed to be heavily invested in teen sex and that he was Executive Coordinator of the Student Guidance and Counseling Administration. Another thing that I thought about was that he must have more than his state salary coming in to support the life-style he maintained. In Massachusetts that's not unusual. In Massachusetts people don't do state work for the salary. It's the fringe benefits—rapine and pillage—that attracts the best and the brightest here.

CHAPTER TWENTY

Susan and I lay in bed in her house on Thanksgiving morning. It was sunny outside the window, and it looked like it wouldn't be cold. I looked at the bedside clock. 7:35. No sound. The room was whitewashed and furnished with colonial pine, and the full flood of sunlight made it almost dazzling in its simple brightness.

Susan said, 'You think it's too early to open the champagne?'

'We could mix it with orange juice and argue for vitamins,' I said.

Susan took my hand under the covers and we lay quietly on our backs amongst the flowered sheets and pillows. 'What does Hawk do on Thanksgiving?' Susan said.

'I have no idea,' I said. 'Probably has honey-roasted pheasant served to him by an Abyssinian maiden with a dulcimer.'

'You are peculiar,' Susan said. 'You trust Hawk with your life or mine. You expect him to risk his life for you—I know you'd risk yours for him—and you don't even know what he does on Thanksgiving. Did you think about inviting him out for dinner?'

'Hawk?' I said.

'Yes.'

'Have Hawk for Thanksgiving dinner?'

'Certainly. Doesn't he have holidays?'

'Suze,' I said. 'You just don't have Hawk for Thanksgiving dinner.'

'Why not?'

'Well, it's . . .' I tried to think of the right way to say it. Hawk and I both knew and we knew without having to say it or even think it. 'You know how in medieval landscape painting the artist would often include an allegorical representation of death to remind us that it is always present and imminent?'

She nodded.

'That's like inviting Hawk to Thanksgiving dinner. He'd be the figure in the landscape, and that would compromise him. Hawk would not want you to invite him.'

'That doesn't make any sense,' Susan said.

'It would to Hawk,' I said.

Susan was quiet, her hand in mine, our bodies close together. Then she said, 'It's where you lose me, this arcane male thing. It's like a set of rituals from a religion that no longer exists, the rules of a kingdom that disappeared before memory. It can't be questioned or explained, it simply is—like gravity or inertia.'

'I know,' I said.

'I realize it's a source of strength for you,' she said, and turned her head from profile to full face, lying close to mine on the pillow, 'but you pay a high price for it too, and so does Hawk.'

'Hawk higher than I do,' I said.

'Because of me?'

'Yes. I have you. He has no one.'

'He has you,' she said.

I said, 'He and I are part of the same cold place. You aren't. You're the source of warmth. Hawk has none. You're what makes me different from Hawk.'

'How different?' she said. Close to me her eyes were enormous.

'I'm here for Thanksgiving dinner,' I said.

'Yes,' she said. 'You are. Let's get to it.'

I said nothing about Mitchell Poitras and Amy Gurwitz and the Department of Education. It was just Susan and me today, and I would wait till tomorrow for anything else.

Susan started the coffee and I built a large fire in the den. We squeezed a small pitcher of orange juice and shared it while I mixed up some johnnycake batter and dropped spoonfuls of it onto the hot griddle. Johnnycake is made with white cornmeal and is somewhere between cornmeal mush and a pancake. It may be an acquired taste, but Suze and I were nothing on a holiday if not authentic. We ate the johnnycake with butter and maple syrup in front of the fire in the den and drank coffee.

'Pilgrims,' I said.

'Speak for yourself, John,' she said.

'Did you know that Priscilla Alden's maiden name was Mullins?' I said.

'Incredibly, no,' Susan said.

'Or that a guy writing at the time referred to Miles Standish as Captain Shrimp?'

'Much like yourself,' Susan said, and grinned at me that fallen-angel grin—the one that Eve must have grinned at Adam.

'Ah,' I said, 'how quickly they forget.'

The fire settled more densely, the logs feeding each other's intensity like mutual enemies. The newspaper came. Susan got both the *Globe* and the *Herald-American*. We took turns reading through them, Susan much more quickly than I. We fueled the fire once or twice and returned to the couch in front of it, feet up on the old sea chest that

138

Susan used as a coffee table, spines bent, sprawled on the cushions with our thighs touching in warm torpor.

Susan went to shower. I asked her not to use all the hot water. She said she wouldn't. I read the sports page. Already, barely a month after the World Series, there was talk of a baseball strike. There were ten contract renegotiations. The Red Sox had decided not to pay anyone, and everyone was threatening to be a free agent. It read like *The Wall Street Journal*. If I were a player, would I want six trillion dollars? Yes. I guessed I would. Did I find it interesting? No, I did not. Has the game changed? Say it ain't so, Joe.

Susan appeared in half an hour wearing jeans no tighter than the skin on a grape and a white oxford shirt with a button-down collar and cowboy boots, smelling of perfume and shampoo and soap. I inhaled. 'Sensual,' I said, 'but not too far from innocence.'

'Far enough,' Susan said. I went to shower and shave and put on clean clothes. When I came back we went to the kitchen and began Thanksgiving dinner. Johnny Hartman was on the stereo. The sun was halfway to zenith and made the tile kitchen glisten. The cooking steamed the windows a bit, filtering the sun slightly and making the brilliance of the kitchen a bit muted as we progressed. At noon Susan brought out a bottle of Dom Pérignon 1971, which we shared as we cooked. The barrel-bodied Lab appeared at the back door and scratched to come in. Susan put down a bowl of water and she drank noisily and long. When she finished she looked expectantly at Susan, her ears a little forward, her tail in a slow scimitar wag. Susan took a round dog biscuit from a box in the cupboard and gave it to the Lab.

'Just one,' she said. 'You're on a diet.' The dog took the biscuit to the other side of the kitchen, wolfed it down, and lay down with a heavy exhalation and a solid thump. She lay on her side against the back door with her feet toward us and her tongue out and appeared to go to sleep.

'Whose dog is that?' I said.

'People down the street.'

By two o'clock dinner was nearly done, and Susan went to set the table while I did the last few tricks, and at 2:30 we sat down to dinner in Susan's dining room with a white linen tablecloth and pink linen napkins and champagne in a silver cooler. It was Susan's good English china and the silver she'd gotten for a wedding present from her ex-mother-in-law. The tall tulip-shaped champagne glasses I had bought her. I'd bought four, but mostly we used just two and drank champagne alone. Sonny Rollins was spinning softly in the background. We didn't insist on complete authenticity.

We began by eating hot pumpkin soup and then some cold asparagus with green herb mayonnaise on a bed of red lettuce. After that we each had half a pheasant with raspberry vinegar sauce and a kind of saffron pilaf that Susan made from white and wild rice with pignolia nuts. For dessert we had sour cherry cobbler with Vermont cheddar cheese, and after we had finished with the last of the champagne and I had embarrassed myself with a second serving, we took coffee and Grand Marnier into the den and drank it in a near stupor on the couch before the dwindling fire with the football game on the television. Susan hated football, so we turned the sound off. She had three back issues of *The New Yorker* and read a series on psychoanalysis that had run there, or pretended to, while I watched the Lions and the Packers, or pretended to. With a last desperate effort I got some more wood on the fire and then settled back on the couch. In fifteen minutes Susan's head rested against my shoulder, her mouth slightly open and

141

her breath shifting occasionally into a faint snore. Before halftime my chin was against my chest and my cheek was pressed against the top of Susan's head.

It was dark when we woke up. The fire barely shimmered on the hearth. A newscast was progressing silently on the TV screen and Thanksgiving Day was nearly past. They ran the local college and high school football results on a crawl, and as the mesmerizing sequence went on it was like a rehearsal of small-town Massachusetts: clean-lined white buildings around a common, square brick schools, cheerleaders with pony-tails and chunky thighs, and parents in pride and contentment watching the children play.

'Nice day,' Susan murmured.

'For some,' I said.

'Not for most?'

'Pretty to think so,' I said.

CHAPTER TWENTY-ONE

We were having leftover cherry cobbler for breakfast on Friday morning when I asked Susan about Mitchell Poitras.

'Oh, sure,' she said. 'I know Mitch.'

'He's living in a very expensive town house on Beacon Street with Amy Gurwitz,' I said.

'Poitras?' Susan said. It always irked me when she called people by their last name. One of the boys. Tough as a ten-minute egg. Wasn't my job to tell her how to talk, so I sat on the irksomeness.

'The very same,' I said. 'And he has a studio and lab set up for making porn films and tapes of very young girls and boys.'

'Poitras?'

'*Mitchell* Poitras,' I said. 'I gather he hadn't put that down in his curriculum vitae.'

'My God, are you sure?'

'Yep.'

'How do you know for sure?' she said.

'I burgled his house Wednesday while he and Amy were off celebrating the harvest.'

'But how did you think ... yes, of course, because that's where you found Amy and she used to be a friend of April's and you had nothing else to do. Why in hell didn't you mention him to me before?'

'Until I found evidence that he worked for the Department of Education I had no reason to think you might know him,' I said.

'Mitchell Poitras?' *Better* I thought. 'But, Jesus Christ, do you realize who he is?'

'Letters say he's Executive Coordinator,

comma, Student Guidance and Counseling Administration.'

Susan nodded.

'It's a job that gives him access to every disturbed kid in the state—access to psychological profiles, teacher reports, principal evaluations, guidance recommendations, often police material. My good sweet Jesus,' Susan said. Her mind could integrate very swiftly.

'What big teeth you have, Granny,' I said.

'Yes,' she said. 'Like finding out your baby-sitter is a werewolf. You say he has facilities to make these things?'

'Yes. Not just a collector, a producer. A distributor.'

'A collector would be bad enough,' Susan said.

'Now, my dear, consenting adults in the privacy of their home . . .'

'Not for a man doing what he does. That's bullshit if you're Poitras. But to produce . . . could it be the wrong man?'

'Ugly fat guy,' I said, 'dresses like he's got a charge at Woolworth's.'

Susan nodded. Her face was sharp with concern. 'What are you going to do?'

'Eventually I'm going to blow the whistle on him, but first I want to see if he knows where April is.'

'Eventually?'

'I didn't hire on to clean up the state,' I said. 'I hired on to find April. First things first.'

'But—'

'No,' I said. 'Don't give me the well-being-of-the-many-against-the-one-speech.   The many are an abstraction. April is not. She rode in my car. I'm going to find her first.'

'One of the rules,' Susan said. There was no smile when she said it.

'Sure,' I said.

'How much is it for April?' she said. 'How much for you?'

'Doesn't matter,' I said. 'It's a way to live. Anything else is confusion.'

Susan sat and looked into her coffee cup. 'I disapprove,' she said.

I nodded.

'But it's yours. There are things you disapprove of that I do anyway,' she said.

I nodded again.

'So first you find April, and then you...' She made a twisting gesture with her right hand, turning the palm up and quickly down again.

'Then I air out the Student Guidance and Counseling Administration,' I said.

'Yes,' she said. 'And in the meantime I might do some research.'

'See whether Poitras recruits?' I said.

She nodded.

'I'll bet he does,' I said.

She nodded again.

CHAPTER TWENTY-TWO

By Monday night we knew that Poitras almost certainly recruited, and on a pretty good scale. I spent Monday staring alertly at his town house on Beacon Street. Susan spent Monday on the phone to people she knew in high school guidance offices around the state. In nearly every case of a dropout, male or female, there was clear evidence of contact with Poitras.

'Either he met the students during crisis intervention sessions,' Susan said to me on the telephone, 'or at coordinative evaluation conferences or he's been a resource person during attempts at therapeutic redirection.'

'You are, I hope, quoting,' I said.

'You mean the jargon? You hear it so much you get used to it.'

'Talking like that will rot your teeth,' I

said.

'Never mind that. I checked back in my own files on Amy Gurwitz and April Kyle. He talked with both of them not long before they dropped out.'

'How long?'

'Well, it's hard to say,' Susan said. 'A kid doesn't just one day drop out. First he or she starts to cut classes and that increases in frequency and after a while it blends into having left school. He spoke to both of them within two weeks of the missing persons report to the Smithfield police—that we could be precise about.'

'How usual is that?' I said.

'That a man in Poitras's position would talk with the students?'

'Yeah.'

'It's not improbable,' Susan said. 'But it's not entirely routine, either. Most people at the state level have no contact at all with students.'

'An educator's dream,' I said.

'Counseling reports and S.I.J.'s are routinely sent to his office,' Susan said, 'but the amount of personal contact is sort of unusual. But not so you'd comment on it unless you discovered that your experience was typical—you know, that he was doing this everywhere.'

'What is an S.I.J.?' I said.

'Student-in-jeopardy forms.'

'Ah, of course,' I said.

'So Poitras, assuming that my sample is representative, had a ready list of children ready to drop out of school, beset with emotional problems, vulnerable to anyone who'd want to exploit them.'

'Chance of a lifetime,' I said. 'King of the chicken flicks.'

'He mustn't be allowed to continue,' Susan said.

'Soon,' I said. 'April will show up soon.'

'I cannot wait too much longer,' she said. 'I cannot permit this to go on.'

'The end of the week,' I said. 'If she doesn't show up by then we'll blow the whistle on Poitras and I'll look elsewhere for April.'

Susan agreed and I hung up and went to bed.

Tuesday morning I was back out on Beacon Street and Tuesday afternoon there came April Kyle. She was wearing a man's army field jacket with a first cavalry patch on it and she looked sort of bedraggled, as if she'd been sleeping in subways and eating light. She slouched along Beacon Street from the direction of Kenmore Square, reading the numbers of the buildings until she reached Poitras's. She stopped for a minute and stared at it, then she went up and rang the bell. The door opened and she went in. I stayed put. Maybe she was just passing through. Maybe just a visit and then back home to Park Street Under. Some cocoa and a Twinkie, a little talk of boys and sock hops, thumb through the yearbook, giggle, maybe a stroll down to the malt shop, or maybe not. *Bare ruined choirs where late the sweet birds sang.*

April didn't come out again. Poitras waddled home at his usual time and let himself in with his key. Still no one came out. I walked three blocks up to Boylston Street and found a public phone and called Susan.

'April's in with Amy and Poitras,' I said. 'What do you think?'

'Stay there. I'll come in. We'll talk to her together.'

'No,' I said. 'I don't want you involved. This deal is tied into some really bad folks, and I don't want them to know your name.'

'I have as much right to be frightened as you do,' Susan said.

'Suze,' I said. 'There've been threats made. By people who can back them up.'

149

'I have the right to be threatened too,' Susan said. 'I'm coming in.'

'No.'

'Yes. You have no right to protect me against my will. I have the right to my own pride and my own self-respect. This is the ugliest piece of business I've ever seen. I'm involved. I got you involved and I want to be part of ending it.'

'Jesus Christ,' I said.

'And if April has to go wee wee again,' Susan said, 'I can go with her.'

'Corner of Fairfield and Beacon,' I said. 'I'll look for you in about twenty minutes. Bitch.'

'Gracefully,' Susan said. 'You give in so gracefully.'

I hung up. It was dark and wet as I walked back down Fairfield. A mixture of rain and snow slopped down, making the street glisten in the streetlights and causing the top of the Prudential and Hancock buildings to disappear in the haze and swirl of it. The commuter traffic had largely drained out of the Back Bay by now—it was twenty of seven, and few people were about on foot. There was a spectral quality to the city. The mist that hovered forty stories up reflected the city lights back in a muted glow, and

150

everything looked a little moonie.

At about quarter past seven I saw Susan walking up Beacon toward me. She had on a poplin trench coat and a large felt hat. The heels of her boots made a clear firm sound in the hushed pale evening. The street seemed somehow to organize around her. Wherever she was she was the focal point, or maybe it just seemed that way because she was my focal point. *No way to decide that. If a tree falls in the forest with no one to hear it, does it make a sound?* She crossed Fairfield and stopped beside me.

'Has anyone ever told you,' I said, 'that you coalesce reality?'

'No. They only say that I'm good in the sack.'

'They are accurate but limited,' I said. 'And if you give me their names I'll kill them.'

'Is April still in there?'

I nodded. 'Unless she slipped out while I was calling you, and why should she?'

'Do we just go knock on the door?'

'Sure,' I said. 'They've got plenty to hide, but they don't know we know it.'

We mounted Poitras's three steps and rang his doorbell. The porch light went on. Amy opened the door. I was wearing a pair of thick-soled Herman survivor boots in deference to the weather and I slipped one of them quietly across the threshold.

Susan said, 'Hello, Amy, remember me?'

Amy looked out closely at Susan and then at me. She remembered me too. 'Hello, Mrs. Silverman, I didn't recognize you at first,' Amy said.

'You know Mr. Spenser,' Susan said.

Amy nodded. She glanced once back over her shoulder.

'May we come in?' Susan said.

Amy looked back over her shoulder again. Then back at us. I smiled. Friendly. From the house behind Amy a voice said, 'Who is it, Amy?'

It was a deep, harsh voice, a growl almost. Poitras appeared in the doorway behind Amy.

'What do you need,' he said in his ferocious voice. His bulk filled the doorway, and I realized he was one of those fat guys who had gotten confused about size as opposed to strength, the way he held himself, the self-consciousness of his looming posture in the doorway. He had gotten a lot of mileage out of bullying people with his size.

Susan said, 'Hello, Mitchell.'

He looked at us the same way Amy had,

152

and then he recognized Susan. 'Susan Silverman. What the hell do you want?'

'We'd like to come and talk, Mitch.'

'About what?'

'About Amy,' Susan said, 'and April Kyle.'

'Get the hell out of here,' Poitras said, and slammed the door on my Herman survivor. Which did what it was there to do. It stopped the door ajar. I was always careful not to do that when I was wearing my Nikes.

'Mitch, let us in,' Susan said.

'Get your foot out of the door,' Poitras said in his scary voice, 'or I'll chop your balls off.'

I looked at Susan. 'Wouldn't that make you mad?' I said.

She didn't smile. She was intent on other things. Poitras shoved on the door. 'Here we go,' I said to Suze.

I put my right hand against the doorjamb and my left hand along the edge of the partly open door and slowly spread my arms. Poitras gave ground. The door opened wide enough for me to get my body in. When I did that, I got my back against the doorjamb and both hands on the half-open door and shoved. The door opened wide and Poitras stumbled back a step into his lavish front hall. I went in after him and Susan came after me. Poitras caught his balance and stretched his right arm out at me and pointed with his index finger.

'You fuck with me,' he said, 'and I'll blow you away.'

'Darth Vadar,' I said. 'That's who you sound like. Darth Vadar. Scary as hell.'

Poitras jabbed his finger at me again. 'I'm warning you.'

He had on a white wash-and-wear shirt with his flowered tie unknotted and hanging down. There was no gun in sight, and he had no special reason to be carrying one, or, if he did, to have it concealed. The threat to blow me away was probably not literal. Still . . .

'Better safe than sorry,' I said to Susan.

I did a little shuffle inside step and hit Poitras a good sharp left hook on the chin. It knocked him down. While he was down, I got his arm twisted up behind him and helped him toward his feet. When he was back up, I shoved him against the wall face first and patted him down with my free hand. No gun. I let him go and stepped away.

'Mitchell,' I said, 'I can do that anytime I want to, and much harder. So stop trying to scare me to death and we'll go into your living room and sit down and'—I made an expostulating gesture by rolling hands—

'communicate.' I smiled at him.

Poitras's face had gotten very dark and his breath seemed short. I couldn't tell if it was passion or exhaustion. He was in dismal shape, but I'd been doing all the heavy work.

'Susan, you're going to have a lot of explaining to do about this. Who is this goon anyway?'

'Mr. Spenser, Mitchell,' Amy said. Her voice was as careful and artificial and unalive as it had been every other time she'd spoken in front of me. For all her voice showed, I had just given Poitras a Popsicle.

'Well, you better have a good explanation,' Poitras said. His breathing was still thick. He turned and went toward the living room, his belly preceding him like the cowcatcher on a locomotive.

When we were in the living room, Amy said, 'May I get you a drink?' She spoke first to Susan and then to me. We both declined.

Poitras remained standing, so did Susan. I could see she wasn't going to sit and let Poitras loom over her. I didn't care. I sat.

'You're really off base on this one, Susan,' Poitras said. The persistency of habit. He was still trying to bully her with his bulk. It's hard to scare the other side when the other side has just knocked you on your ass. Even if

155

I hadn't hit him, I had learned some time ago that Susan was difficult to bully.

'This is really unprofessional, Susan. I can't believe you. This is way, way off base,' Poitras said. He didn't look at me.

Susan stepped closer to him. Fat as he was, he wasn't very tall, and in her high-heeled boots she was almost eye level. 'Shut up,' she said. The words cracked with energy. 'I am not interested either in your clichés about professionalism or your pathetic Bluto act. I am here to talk with April Kyle and I will do so right now.' She turned her head at Amy Gurwitz and snapped, 'Go get her.'

It was Mrs. Silverman the guidance teacher. In reflex Amy turned and started from the room.

Poitras said, 'Amy,' and she stopped. Two authority figures could play Ping-Pong with her.

Susan's voice shimmered with intensity as she spoke to Poitras. 'Do not be a bigger asshole than you are, Mitchell—get her. Bring her out here. Or there be real trouble.'

I shook my head slightly at Susan. Unless we wanted the cops to come right now, it was better if Poitras didn't know what we knew. I didn't want him covering his tracks before we nailed him.

Poitras glanced at me from the corner of his eye and looked quickly away.

'I saw her come in, Fats,' I said. 'Either you bring her out or I'll go room by room through the place till I find her.'

'You can't do that,' Poitras said, and glared at me.

'Yes I can. I proved it a minute ago in the hall. Bring her out.'

Poitras glared harder. 'Someone ought to blow you right out of the water,' he said.

'That may be true. But it'll have to be someone in better shape than you.'

Poitras looked back at Susan. 'Last chance,' she said.

I knew that Poitras didn't want me going through the house.

'Okay,' he said. 'But I don't want you people harassing her. She came to me in desperation, and I don't want her upset.'

'Really care about the kids, don't you, Mitch?' Susan said.

'You're goddamned right I do,' Poitras said. 'Somebody's got to.'

CHAPTER TWENTY-THREE

April came into the room. She had taken off the fatigue jacket and was dressed as I'd last seen her in the dark woods at the edge of Route 95, except that her clothes looked a little shabbier. She looked at Susan and said, 'What are you doing here?'

'I've come to see you,' Susan said.

'I'm not going back,' April said.

'You don't have to go back,' Susan said. 'I only wish to know that you are all right and that you are in a situation that is supportive.'

'Shit,' April said. 'That's teacher shit. Supportive.'

'Your parents want you back,' Susan said.

'I'll bet,' April said.

'They do. They hired Mr. Spenser to find you. Doesn't that tell you something?'

'My father?'

'What about him?'

'He wants me back?'

'I don't think he knows what he wants,' Susan said. 'Part of him doesn't want you back. Part of him surely does. Unfortunately it's the negative part that shows.'

'He don't want me back.'

158

'He's confused,' Susan said. 'He's in pain. He doesn't know how to say what he feels.'

'I know how he feels. He thinks I'm shit. He thinks I'm a whore. Well, fuck him, you know? I'm not going back.'

'And your mother,' Susan said.

'She's a wimp. She just sucks around him.'

'Do you want to stay here then?'

'Yes.'

'Why?'

April shrugged. 'Why not? It's a nice place. I've crashed in a lot worse, you know?'

'This is not a place for you, April. You don't have to go home. I can't force you and I wouldn't if I could. But not here.'

'Why not?'

Susan looked straight at Poitras when she spoke. 'Because this is an absolute pig of a man,' she said.

April laughed, a harsh little sound, without humor. 'So what?' she said.

Amy Gurwitz was sitting quietly on a hassock in front of an easy chair near the French doors. Her knees and ankles were together. Her hands were clasped in her lap. She was watching the activity as if it were a movie and she was enthralled.

Susan looked at me. She was stuck. So was I.

'We can take her by force, Suze,' I said. 'But what are we going to do with her?'

'She came here looking for some help,' Poitras said. 'I was the only one she could trust. So she came here. I'll step around that crack about me being a pig, and I'm giving it to you straight. She's welcome here as long as she wants. Just like Amy, and you can make whatever you want out of that with your dirty goddamned minds, all of you. But the kids know who they can count on, by God. So whyn't you and your goon get the hell out of here before you just make things worse.'

'Is that G-O-O-N, rhymes with noon?' I said. 'Or G-U-N-E, rhymes with prune?'

Susan was looking at Poitras and he back at her. Then he looked away. Another point for Susan. She had all the points but he seemed to have April. Was it time to play the porno hand. I didn't think April would care. Probably admire his artistic interests. We could bust Poitras, but what would Amy and April do then? Did April go back to Red, maybe take Amy along? I knew she wouldn't go home. They might very well be better off with Poitras than with Red.

'This is not over, Mitchell,' Susan said. 'I will not give in on this. I can't. I can't let you have access to children.'

'Suze,' I said, and made a time-out sign by putting one hand horizontally on top of the other one held vertical. 'Time to go. I told April I wouldn't force her, and I won't.'

Susan opened her mouth and closed it and looked at me once and then turned on her heel and walked out. I stood, smiled at Amy and April, and started toward the door.

'No thanks,' I said to Poitras, 'we'll find our way out. Nice seeing you again, April. Amy. Mitchell, I may stop by sometime and knock you on your ass again.' Then I followed Susan.

Walking down Beacon Street, Susan was galvanic with fury. 'How can we let him keep her. Them? How can we?'

'Hey, Suze,' I said, 'why nip a budding film career?'

'Goddamn it,' Susan said, 'it is not funny.'

CHAPTER TWENTY-FOUR

'Where you parked?' I said.

'Commonwealth.'

'Want a snack before we part?'

She nodded and we walked up toward Newbury Street.

'How does a slob like that get to be executive nitwit, or whatever he is, in the state education system?' I said.

'Knew someone, I suppose,' Susan said. 'There's all sorts of hiring regulations and elaborate interviewing procedures, and one call from practically anyone circumvents it. Half the jobs in the Commonwealth are bagged before they're advertised.'

'Hard to imagine Poitras has a friend,' I said.

'He has girls and dirty movies,' Susan said.

I looked at her in the odd light, under the high mist. 'Cynical,' I said. 'Beautiful but hard, like a diamond.'

'It would be a way to make friends,' Susan said.

'True,' I said. 'It would also be a way to put someone in your debt if you had supplied him with things that public servants aren't supposed to want.'

We turned down Newbury.

'How about the police?' Susan said.

'And what happens to April and Amy?'

Susan nodded. We crossed Fairfield. The rain was misting down now, steady but very fine. The temperature had risen.

'On the other hand,' Susan said, 'what happens to them in any case?'

162

'I was hoping you'd think of something,' I said.

'Maybe there isn't anything to think of. We could get them back home. But that's where they learned to be what they are.'

We crossed Exeter Street and went into the Bookstore Cafe. There were books, and there was blond woodwork, and a bar and tables, and in the back a balcony as well. I liked eating in there. It made me feel intellectual.

I had a tongue sandwich on rye and Susan had a salad. We split a bottle of Norman cider. Not everybody sells Norman cider by the bottle.

'Has a European feel,' Susan said.

'That sounds terrific,' I said. 'Can I have one?'

Susan grinned at me. 'How did you ever get to be so big without growing up?' she said.

'Iron self-control,' I said.

For dessert we had one Linzer torte and two forks and I walked Susan to her car. Before she got in she leaned her forehead against mine. 'We really do have to think of something to do about Poitras and those girls.'

'Yes.'

She kissed me lightly on the mouth and

climbed into the front seat of her big Ford Bronco.

'I never figured how you do that without giving me a flash of thigh.'

She grinned again at me. 'Iron self-control,' she said, and started up the Bronco and drove off. I stood and watched the car as long as it stayed in sight, three blocks down Commonwealth and then a left turn onto Berkeley and out of sight across the intersection. I always felt a little sad when she left, or when I left. Even if it wasn't for long. Even if I'd see her tomorrow. Probably kept it fresh. Probably drive each other wacko if we were together all the time. Sure we would. Better to both have our own place and do our own stuff and be together when we chose to.

I walked back up Commonwealth toward Fairfield. Very sensible, I thought. Stay separate and together. I crossed Commonwealth and went down Fairfield in the bright soaking mist. It's the right way . . . except how come I miss her whenever I leave her? My car had a ticket on it. Crime doesn't pay. Justice never sleeps.

Neither did I when I got home, or at least it didn't feel much like I slept. Except I must have, because I was having dreams that had something to do with being with Susan and

164

not being with her and trying to find some children. I woke up and fell asleep and dreamed variations of the same dream until the phone rang and got me up at 7:15. It was Susan.

'You better come out here, right now,' Susan said, and there was no laughter in her voice.

'Trouble?'

'They've killed the dog,' Susan said. 'Please come quickly.'

It was pre-rush hour, and what traffic there was was going the other way. I was at her house in twenty-five minutes. Susan met me at her front door. She had on her warm-up suit and sneakers. Without makeup her face looked a little simpler, like she must have as a kid.

'In the kitchen,' she said. Her eyes were wet.

I went in. The black Lab was there. It had been shot in the head and the blood was stiff and dry and nearly as black as the fur it had stiffened. Some had soaked into the rug where the dog lay, on its side, between the kitchen table and the back door. I moved its leg. It was unyielding. The body had stiffened.

'You find it this morning?'

165

'Yes.'

'You come into the kitchen last night?'

Susan shook her head. 'I came in the front door and went right upstairs.'

'Probably shot it last night. Probably thought she was yours. Your back door wasn't locked.'

'No,' Susan said. 'You know I don't lock the doors.'

I stood up. 'You may as well call the cops, and the dog officer.'

'She was a lovely dog,' Susan said. 'What will I tell her folks?'

I didn't say anything.

'Why?' Susan looked at me. 'You mentioned there had been threats, but . . . ?'

'I don't know. Maybe a warning. Maybe a substitute. They came and you weren't here, but the dog was, so they brought her in and shot her instead. It won't happen again,' I said.

'You know who did it?'

'I know who had it done. That's better. Call the cops.'

CHAPTER TWENTY-FIVE

Two cops came with the local dog officer. One of the cops was Cataldo. They took the dog away and the other cop went to tell the owners. Susan told Cataldo she didn't know why someone would do this.

Cataldo looked at me. 'And you wouldn't have any idea either, would you?'

'No.'

'Funny thing to do for no reason. Not even your dog, Susan.'

'I know, Lonnie. I know. The poor thing. Maybe they were burglars and thought the dog would give them away.'

'So they brought it in and shot it?'

Susan shrugged.

I said, 'I have to go to work. Can you keep an eye on her?'

Cataldo nodded. 'I'll take her to school and pick her up when she's ready to come home.'

'How about after that?' I said.

'I'll stick around,' Cataldo said. ''Case the burglars come back.'

'How about a paid detail?' I said. 'Until I get this straightened out.'

Cataldo shook his head. 'I know Susan a

long time now. Most of the guys do. We'll watch her for free.'

'Who wouldn't?' I said.

Cataldo nodded again.

Susan said, 'I won't even argue,' and they went together in the cruiser.

I stood in her kitchen looking at the bloodstained rug and called Henry Cimoli on the phone.

'Tell Hawk I need him,' I said. 'I'll be in there in about half an hour and I want him as soon as he can get there.'

Henry said, 'I'll tell him.' And I hung up and headed for my car. When I got to the Harbor Health Club, Henry was in his office and Hawk was with him. They were drinking coffee. Henry had on blue-striped Adidas sneakers and a white T-shirt and dark blue sweat pants with zippered bottoms. The T-shirt said MANAGER in blue letters. Hawk was wearing gray and black Puma running shoes, white denim jeans, and a white cashmere sweater, V-neck, with no shirt under it.

'Coffee?' Henry said. He was a little guy who'd been a very fine lightweight fighter once. Now he managed the Harbor Health Club and worked out twice a day. He looked like a superman doll. I took a white china mug of coffee from him. Hawk was slouched

168

in one of the guest chairs, his feet on the desk, holding a coffee mug in both hands.

To Hawk I said, 'Somebody shot a dog and left it in Susan's kitchen.'

'She okay?'

'Yes. I figured Tony Marcus.'

Hawk nodded. He took a sip of coffee, put the mug on Henry's desk, and stood up by letting his feet drop off the desk and levering his body up as his feet hit. 'Let's get to it,' he said.

'You know where to find him?' I said.

'Yeah, he got a place in the South End—restaurant called Buddy's Fox, Clarendon and Tremont.'

Henry said, 'You want a third?'

I said, 'No. Anything goes bad, tell Quirk, and see about Susan.'

Henry nodded. Hawk slid open a drawer in Henry's desk and took out a shoulder holster with a .357 Magnum in it. He shrugged it on and put on a sand-colored suede jacket with a zipper front. And we went.

Buddy's Fox was across from the big round-roofed performing arts center. Hawk parked his black Jaguar sedan at a hydrant in front of the restaurant and we got out. Hawk opened the trunk and took out a twelve-gauge shotgun. A pump model. He checked the action once, and then fed five shells into the magazine. He closed the trunk and said, 'The restaurant is long and no wider than the front. Booths on both sides. Bar across the back. To the right of the bar is a little corridor. Down the corridor there are the men's room, the ladies' room on the right wall, the kitchen door at the far end, and Tony's office door on the left wall.'

Hawk held the shotgun casually across his shoulder, trigger guard up, as if we were shooting grouse on the moors.

'He always in there taking care of business. Has breakfast here every morning. Leaves after supper every night.'

'He ever alone,' I said.

'No,' Hawk said. There was a sign in the restaurant window that said OPEN FOR BREAKFAST. I took my gun out and let it hang by my side. We went in. The place was old and looked as though it had been kept that way. There were four or five people having breakfast. Behind the bar at the far end a big, thick-necked black man with a flat nose was polishing glasses. We were halfway down the length of the room before he noticed us, and another ten steps toward him before he registered the shotgun. He looked toward the archway at the end of the bar and then put down the glass he was polishing and let his hands drop.

I raised my gun, 'If your hands disappear, Jack, you're dead,' I said.

The bartender froze. 'Put 'em on the bar,' I said. The bartender put both hands on the bar. The breakfast crowd was beginning to notice that all was not copacetic. The sounds of cutlery and conversation died. Without lifting the shotgun off his shoulder, Hawk stepped around behind the bar and hit the bartender in the forehead, bringing the gun butt forward as if he were driving a peg. The sound was harsh in the now dead-silent room. The bartender slumped off the bar and fell without a sound. I went past the end of the bar down the corridor. Hawk came behind me. A waitress met us halfway down the short hall. She had a tray of ham and eggs and home fries and toast.

I said, 'Go back in the kitchen, honey, and be quiet.'

She looked at the gun in my hand and past me at Hawk with his shotgun and backed down the hall and into the kitchen. Just short of the swinging door on the left wall was a paneled oak door with no marking.

Hawk nodded. I turned the knob. It was locked.

A voice inside said, 'Yeah. Who is it?'

Hawk moved up beside me. 'Hawk,' he said. 'Open up.'

A lock clicked, the knob turned, and Hawk and I hit the door simultaneously, each with a shoulder. The door rammed open, and whoever had opened it went backward and fell over a chair. Inside I kicked the door shut behind us. Hawk stepped to the left of the door, pumped a shell into the chamber of the shotgun, and held the gun level and still. To my left the guy who'd opened the door was getting to his feet. There was a trickle of blood from his nose. Another man stood against the back wall of the office, his hands straight at his sides and slightly spread. At the desk in front of me, with the remnants of breakfast on a tray and a white napkin tucked into his collar, was Tony Marcus. He was a nice-looking guy with a salt-and-pepper Afro and a thick mustache. He was tan skinned, not nearly as dark as Hawk. His neck and chin line looked soft and comfortable. The suit he had on under the napkin looked like maybe a thousand dollars and custom tailored. His nails shone.

He looked at me and Hawk without any expression. Then he shook his head. 'Hawk,' he said sadly, 'siding with him against us?

Turning on a brother?' He shook his head again. Hawk was whistling softly between his teeth. A jazzy Yankee Doodle.

I spoke to the two bodyguards. 'On the floor,' I said. 'Face down.' The two men lay face down. 'Clasp your hands behind your neck,' I said. 'And keep them there. If either one of you moves, I'll kill you.' Then I put my gun back in my hip holster and said to Marcus, 'Step around here in front of the desk.'

Marcus took the napkin from his collar, wiped his mouth and mustache, dropped the napkin on the tray, and stood up. His face showed only a mild sadness. 'This is too bad,' he said. 'This is very much too bad.'

He walked around the desk and I hit him in the stomach with my left hand and on the point of the chin with my right hand. He went backward against the desk and sagged without falling. I hit him again and he did go down. He tilted left and fell on his side on the floor. The two bodyguards remained motionless. Hawk continued his barely audible whistle. I reached down and got hold of Marcus's lapels with both hands and lifted him upright and sat him on the edge of his desk and held him still. Blood ran down his chin.

'You're about ten seconds from dead,' I said, 'unless I know that never again will anybody go anywhere near Susan Silverman.'

The blood was steady, from a cut inside his mouth probably, and it was ruining his shirt and tie.

'Never heard of her.'

I hit him in the face again, holding his lapel with my left hand to keep him up.

'You sent somebody out there to scare her, or me, or both, because I'm looking around under some of your rocks.'

'Man's crazy, Hawk.' Marcus had trouble saying *crazy*, because his lower lip was starting to puff.

'Probably is,' Hawk said, 'but that don't help you none, Tony.'

Marcus turned back toward me. 'What you after?'

I let go of him and stepped back away from him. Marcus glanced quickly at the door and away. I knew he was waiting for reinforcements.

'Anybody comes in that door, and I'll kill you,' I said. 'So don't be too hopeful.'

'Won't matter,' Marcus said. 'I'm dead. You're dead. Hawk's dead. Won't matter. I didn't get to own what I own by being scared to die.'

'What am I digging up that you don't want dug up?' I said.

Marcus shook his head. 'Take another punch, if you want to. Keep you busy 'fore you die.'

'Okay,' I said. 'You're tough. I'm tough. Hawk's tough. Let's stop for a while being tough and start being smart.'

There was a soft knock on the door. I took my gun out and pushed the muzzle into Marcus's neck. He didn't flinch. A voice outside said 'Tony?' I nodded. Marcus said, 'Yeah, Buster?'

'There's a cop car parked outside, Tony,' Buster said.

Marcus said, 'Go stand behind the bar, Buster. Polish some glasses.'

The blood continued to run down his chin. He made no move to wipe it away.

'What you got in mind?' Marcus said to me.

I put the gun back on my hip and said, 'You got a very fine organization working here. Whores, dope, numbers, cards, horse parlors, bootleg booze, loansharking—did I leave anything out?'

'Protection,' Marcus said. 'Some leg breaking. Shooting.'

'Fun,' I said. 'I'm not out to break that up.

If it's not you, it'll be someone else. I do what I can, not what I should.'

Marcus nodded.

'What I want is Mitchell Poitras and a little kid named April Kyle.'

Marcus shrugged.

'So why do you care?'

Marcus made a small noncommittal gesture with one hand.

'I say you didn't want the Poitras connection exposed. I say you had a nice supply of white suburban teenage whores coming in, and there's always a big demand for them. High-ticket items, you might say. And you found me chasing one of the kids that Poitras recruited, you figured it would be easier to chase me off than to risk the source drying up.'

'Say that's so,' Marcus said. 'So what?'

'It's not easy to chase me off,' I said. 'And it's not going to get easier. You probably got enough bodies finally to get it done, but it won't be easy. You're up against me, and you're up against Hawk.'

'I not sure he do have enough bodies for that,' Hawk said softly.

'If you do, and you burn me, or both of us, then there's some cops that will take it hard, and they'll keep hoisting your pimps and busting up your books and maybe bringing you in once a week for routine questioning. And maybe you'll fall down the stairs when they do. Chasing me off is a mistake. It's nothing but trouble.'

'You got a better idea,' Marcus said.

'I bet he do,' Hawk murmured.

'I take Poitras and the kid and leave you out of it,' I said. 'I can't leave Poitras in place.'

'I don't give a shit about one whore more or less,' Marcus said.

'You know that Poitras makes chicken flicks down there—boys and girls?'

Marcus frowned. 'Boys too?' he said.

'Yeah.'

'I don't deal in that,' Marcus said.

'I take Poitras, and you're out of it.'

'If I don't like it.'

'We do it anyway,' I said. 'And a lot of people get dumped, and your business goes to hell.'

'He talking for you, Hawk?' Marcus said.

'Yep.'

'You with him the whole way?'

'Yep.'

'Would he go that way for your black ass?'

Hawk said, 'Do it, Tony. You don't know him, but you know me. He as hard to kill as I

177

am. And as bad. Do it or he going to fuck up your life.'

'No way you can push me into a deal I don't want,' Marcus said. 'Not with guns or fists or anything else. I don't push.'

'It's a deal that makes sense,' I said.

'I make a deal and I stick to it,' Marcus said. 'Hawk'll tell you that. You make a deal with me and it's dead solid done. You understand. No mistakes, no backing out. I say I'll do something, I do it.'

I looked at Hawk. He nodded.

'I take Poitras and the kid and the kid he lives with. I keep you out of it, and Poitras won't talk because he knows what would happen if he did.'

Marcus nodded.

'And if anyone goes near Susan Silverman I'll kill him. And you.'

Marcus made a movement with his puffed lips that was probably a smile. 'Thought you'd get to that.'

'He's talking for me on that too,' Hawk said.

Marcus nodded. He looked down at the two bodyguards face down on the floor. 'Took Buster easy enough,' he said almost to himself. 'And these two clowns.' He picked up his napkin from the desktop and began to dab at the blood on his chin. 'Not sure you could have pulled it off without the cops outside.' He stopped dabbing with the napkin and held it wadded against his mouth. 'Got some cop in your pocket,' he said, his voice muffled by the napkin. Hawk and I were quiet. Holding the napkin against his mouth, Marcus rolled his neck as if trying to loosen the muscles. Then he looked at me and took the napkin away from his mouth. It was bloody and wet.

'Okay,' he said. 'You make sure Poitras knows what not to talk about. He talks, it's on you.'

'Okay,' I said. 'We clean?'

'Almost,' Marcus said, and hit me an overhand right on the jaw. He rolled off the desk as he threw the punch, and his full weight was behind it. It was a good punch. I had to take a quick backward step to keep from falling.

'Now we're clean,' Marcus said. 'Your lucky day, honky. You and your lady.'

My head was ringing. 'Not bad,' I said. 'Not a bad punch for a pimp.'

CHAPTER TWENTY-SIX

As we walked out through the restaurant Hawk said, 'I seen you slip better punches than that one.' There was no one in the restaurant except Buster, behind the bar, holding ice against his forehead.

'Won't hurt if he feels better about things,' I said.

'We could have zipped him.'

'But then there'd be people trying to zip us. This way is better. It puts Susan out of it, if he'll keep his word.'

'He will,' Hawk said.

In front of the restaurant, as we went out onto Tremont Street, was an unmarked car with the motor idling, and its give-away buggy whip antenna trembling slightly in synch with the engine vibrations.

'That's why no reinforcements came,' I said.

'Henry called Quirk,' Hawk said.

I bent over and looked in the window. Belson sat behind the wheel and Martin Quirk was beside him. Quirk rolled down the window. The smell of Belson's cheap cigar was strong.

'Henry call you?' I said.

'Uh-huh.'

'You down here officially?' I said.

'Nope. Henry told us somebody took a swipe at Susan, and you and your pet shark'—Quirk pointed at Hawk with his chin—'were coming down to talk with Marcus about it.'

Hawk grinned and drifted over to his car and put the shotgun in the trunk.

I said, 'We did. It's all straightened out.' There was a shotgun between Quirk's knees and another one locked upright into the catch on the dashboard. 'Thanks,' I said.

Quirk was immaculate, as he always was. Hair recently cut, face newly shaved. His trench coat just out of the cleaners.

Quirk nodded. Belson chewed his cigar into a more comfortable corner of his mouth.

'Best to Susan,' Quirk said. And the car pulled slowly away and drove Tremont Street.

Hawk was leaning against his car with his arms crossed. I said, 'Let's go.' And Hawk walked around and got into the driver's side.

As we headed back for the Harbor Health Club, Hawk said, 'You tell Henry to do that?'

'No. I told him to let Quirk know if we didn't come back. You were there.'

181

'Not sure how legal that is,' Hawk said, 'cops sitting backup while you and me roust some citizens.'

'About as legal as you and me rousting the citizens,' I said.

'That's what I thought,' Hawk said.

Hawk dropped me at the Health Club and I picked up my car and drove out to Smithfield. I was in Susan's kitchen drinking coffee and eating oatmeal cookies when she came home from school. Cataldo came into the house with her.

'You don't have to watch her anymore,' I said. 'It's been fixed.'

Susan put her coat across the back of a kitchen chair and said to Cataldo, 'Coffee?'

Cataldo shook his head. 'No, thanks. I hope,' he said to me, 'there was no crime committed in fixing things?'

'Cynical and suspicious,' I said. 'Years of police work will do that to you, Suze.'

She was making instant coffee for herself at the counter and her face was serious. She nodded. Cataldo said, 'See you, Susan.'

She said, 'Thank you very much, Lonnie.'

He nodded at me, and Susan walked him to the door. When she came back, she put her arms around my neck from behind as I sat at the table and pressed her cheek against the top of my head for a moment. Then she got her coffee from the counter and came and sat across the table from me. She took a cookie and bit a small half-circle from the edge and sipped some coffee.

'What did you do,' she said, 'to fix it?'

I told her.

'What if Quirk hadn't showed up to cover your back?' Susan said when I got through.

'Can't say, maybe nothing. Maybe we'd have had to shoot some people. No use thinking about what didn't happen.'

'I was scared all day,' Susan said. 'I knew you'd do something like that. I was afraid you'd do it alone. That you wouldn't even ask Hawk.'

'I didn't ask Hawk,' I said. 'He came along uninvited. Like Quirk and Belson.'

She nodded. 'I was scared for you. I was scared you'd be hurt, or killed. And I was scared for me. Scared I'd have to deal with what I know about Poitras alone.'

I nodded. 'Quirk would have helped you,' I said. 'And Frank Belson.'

'You think that Marcus will stick to his bargain?'

'Yes. Hawk says he will.'

'And if Hawk is wrong?'

'Hawk isn't wrong about things like that,' I

said. 'There are things Hawk doesn't know anything about. But what he knows, he knows for certain.'

She nibbled at another cookie. She was wearing a new perfume, and the light from the window behind her made her black hair shine. Seeing her was a tangible physical sensation for me. I could feel the sight of her move through my body. It was always difficult not to touch her.

'We have to decide about Poitras and April and, I suppose, Amy Gurwitz,' I said.

'I know.'

'Busting Poitras will be easy. There's plenty of evidence in the place. Juries and judges are inclined to be unsympathetic to child pornographers, and I imagine the Department of Education frowns upon them as well, at least as far as official policy goes.'

'Yes. I'm sure it does,' Susan said. 'It's the girls.'

'Yeah, it is. I don't know what to do with the goddamned girls.'

There was one cookie left on the plate. I took it and ate it while Susan held her coffee cup to her lips and tapped her bottom teeth slowly against the rim. Then she drank some coffee, put the cup down, and said, 'I don't know either.'

CHAPTER TWENTY-SEVEN

My jaw was very sore where Marcus had hit me. It had stiffened up overnight, and I had to talk through my teeth. I sounded as if I'd just graduated from Harvard.

It didn't impress a vice squad detective named McNeely who sat behind his desk on Berkeley Street and listened while I told him my plan.

'We got nothing better to do than hang around with a handful of warrants and wait for you to give the nod?' he said.

'It's the only way it can go down,' I said. 'It's a deal I made, and I'll stick to it.'

'You made,' McNeely said. 'Who the hell are you? You got information about a porn operation, you give it to me.'

Belson was leaning against a file cabinet beside McNeely's desk. His cigar was burned short, and before he spoke he picked a shred of wet cigar wrapper off his lip.

'For crissake, Tom,' Belson said. 'He's handing you the garbage all wrapped and neat. All you got to do is swing by and pick it up.'

'This ain't homicide, Belson,' McNeely

185

said. 'This is vice. You brought him over and introduced him, you don't need to hang around and kibitz.'

Belson winked at me. 'Must be a slow month on the kickbacks,' Belson said. 'Vice guys are all grouchy.'

McNeely was a thick slouchy man with a bald head. He looked at Belson hard for a long minute. Belson smiled at him. His thin face looking good-humored. A faint blue shadow of his heavy beard already showing, although it was only ten in the morning.

'I'll let that pass, Belson,' he said finally.

'Thought you might,' Belson said.

McNeely looked back at me. 'How do I know you won't blow this?'

'Because I'm good, and this is easy,' I said. 'I didn't have to bring it to you first. I could have done my business and then called nine one one. I'm giving you notice so it'll all be clean. The right papers, that sort of thing. The thing is going to blow statewide, and probably interstate. I could have called in the Staties, or the FBI, and left you sucking hind tit.'

McNeely looked at Belson again. 'He level?' he said.

'He's a real pain in the ass,' Belson said. 'But he does what he says he'll do.'

McNeely was playing with a rubber band, stretching it between the thumb and little finger of his left hand. He leaned back in his swivel chair and examined the stretched elastic. He opened his three middle fingers out and stretched the band into a crude circle and looked at that.

'Okay. I'll go along,' he said. 'You fuck it up and you're out of business. I can promise you that.'

'That's the kind of endorsement I was hoping for,' I said.

'You got it,' McNeely said, and let the rubber band slip off his fingers and skitter across the desktop. 'I'll be waiting to hear from you.'

I nodded and got up, and Belson and I walked out of the squad room.

'Lovable,' I said to Belson as we walked to the elevator.

'Nicest guy in the vice squad,' Belson said.

The elevator came and I went down. It was cold on Berkeley Street. As I walked the three blocks from Police Headquarters to my office the wind was blowing grit around and doing a good job of penetrating my leather trench coat. If I zipped in the pile lining, then the coat was too small. One of those life choices that remind us of reality. Tight or cold. Maybe I should get a new coat. Something to make me look like a young Robert Mitchum. The choices in size 48 were fairly narrow, however. Maybe a young Guinn 'Big Boy' William would be enough.

I sat in my office with my chair swiveled around and looked out the window. I could see a portion of Boylston Street from this position. If I stood up I could look down onto Berkeley Street. On windy days like this I usually liked to stand and look down and watch the skirts swirl on the young women who worked in the insurance companies. But today I was too busy trying to think of what to do about April Kyle when we busted Poitras. She was unlikely to go home, and if she went she was unlikely to stay, and if she stayed it was unlikely to do her any good. Susan said there were some social service organizations that might take her, but what experience I had with them was not encouraging.

Across the street the young art director with the black hair and the good hips was leaning on her drawing board looking out the window. Our eyes met. She grinned and waved. I waved back. We had never met and our relationship was conducted solely through windows across a busy street. Maybe when I got my new coat... The more I thought about April the more I didn't know what to do with her.

Susan was breathing down my neck about Poitras. She was tougher minded, sometimes. To keep Poitras away from next year's crop of burnouts she'd let April go. She was right, of course. The greatest good for the greatest number. Democracy. Western civilization. Humanism. A working definition of ethical behavior.

The mail came through the letter slot. I got up and picked it off the floor. There was nothing in it I wanted to read. I threw it away unopened. I stood at the window with my hands in my hip pockets and looked down into the street. The wind was swirling newspapers and Big Mac wrappers around, but almost all the women from the insurance companies were wearing pants. *Why doesn't the breeze excite me?* I walked across the room and leaned my forearms on my file cabinet and my chin on my forearms. Why didn't I know any nuns? A strong-willed, smiling sister with a sense of humor who looked like Celeste Holm. Sister Flanagan's Girls Town. She ain't heavy, she's my sister. Where the hell is the woman's movement when you need it?

I didn't know any nuns. I didn't even know any priests. I knew some pimps and some leg breakers and some cops and some junkies and some whores and a few madams. Actually I knew one madam.

I could hear the faint chatter of a typewriter from somewhere down the hall and the occasional ping of the steam pipes in my office. I could hear traffic sounds, muffled by the closed window, and in the corridor a pair of high-heeled shoes tapped briskly past my office door.

I knew a madam in New York named Patricia Utley. Or I used to. I straightened up and pulled out the second file drawer in the cabinet. I found a manila folder marked Rabb, in about the right alphabetical sequence, and took it out and brought it to my desk. I riffled through the details of some business I'd done about seven years ago. On a piece of note paper from a Holiday Inn was Patricia Utley's name and address and phone number. I put the file back and sat down at my desk again and called Patricia Utley's number.

A man's voice answered. I asked for Ms. Utley. The voice asked who was calling and I told him. The line clicked on to hold and in maybe thirty seconds I heard her voice.

'Spenser?' she said.

'You remember, then?'

'Yes,' she said. 'Summer, 1975. I remember quite clearly.'

I said, 'I owe you a favor and this isn't going to be it. This is going to be a request for another favor.'

'Um-hum.'

'Are you still in business?' I said.

'Yes.'

'I'd like you to meet a young woman I know. She's interested in a career,' I said.

'Are you working on commission?' Patricia Utley's voice sounded as if she were smiling.

'No.'

'Well, I must say it's a surprising request coming from the man I remember, but yes. I would talk with her.'

'Okay,' I said. 'I don't know exactly when. I'm working on that, but soon. I'll call ahead.'

'Certainly,' she said. 'Have things worked out for the young woman we once had mutual interest in seven years ago?'

'Yes,' I said.

'Good,' she said. 'I'll look forward to seeing you soon.'

We hung up and I sat back and thought some more.

CHAPTER TWENTY-EIGHT

'You're going to encourage her to be a whore?' Susan said. We were at my place, with a fire going, sitting on the couch with our feet on the coffee table.

'It's all she wants to do,' I said. 'At least with Patricia Utley she'll be a high-class whore.'

There was feta cheese and fresh Syrian bread and Kalamata olives and cherry tomatoes and green pepper rings and smoked kielbasa from Karl's Sausage Kitchen on a large platter between our feet. We had opened a bottle of new Beaujolais.

Susan drank some wine. 'You are an original thinker,' she said. 'I'll give you that.'

'Give me a better choice,' I said.

'There are agencies to deal with this sort of thing.'

'Uh-huh. Or maybe a nice foster home?'

'Perhaps,' Susan said. 'Often either of those choices is a good one for a child.'

I always knew when she was speaking professionally. Her language became more formal.

'We did consider the possibility that being

a whore offered her more than she was used to getting.'

'Yes,' Susan said, 'but only in comparison to her home life, to the sterility of her parents and their expectations and the conventional town that reiterated those expectations. Life in Smithfield is not easy unless you are nearly interchangeable with everyone else. Especially in the public schools.'

'Maybe being a whore in fact is better than being a whore to the expectations of your neighborhood,' I said.

Susan shook her head.

'Let me call some people in Youth Services,' she said.

'Sure,' I said. 'Want me to ask Poitras for some names?'

Susan shook her head again and frowned. 'Not fair,' she said. 'There are lots of good people out there. Poitras doesn't represent them all.'

'I know,' I said. 'I guess I am just dysfunctional about institutional solutions.'

We were quiet. I spat an olive pit into the fireplace. It made a barely audible sizzle. I drank some Beaujolais. Then I made a small triangular sandwich out of a piece of Syrian bread and some cheese, with a pepper ring, one cherry tomato, and an olive. I pitted the olive before I slipped it into the sandwich. The proportions are the secret in eating feta cheese and raw vegetables. I sampled the sandwich. Too much cheese obliterated the other flavors. I ate it anyway. Plenty of time to experiment, plenty of time to get it right. I ate some sausage. Susan was swirling the wine about in her glass and watching the small turbulence she'd created.

'Distaste,' I said, 'is our automatic response to prostitution. It's almost impossible for us to think about it beyond deploring it, you know?'

I poured a little more wine in my glass.

'Yes,' Susan said. 'I know. I suppose if you do think about it beyond the normal assumptions you have to recognize that prostitution is not a single experience.'

'No,' I said. 'It isn't. There's lots of kinds of prostitution. Metaphorically the kinds are almost limitless. Everyone who does things for money instead of pride, I suppose.'

Susan smiled at me. 'Didn't I see you building a cabin out by a pond in Concord the other day?'

'Uncle Henry,' I said. 'Not me. He was always a little dippy, Henry was.'

The wine was gone. I got another bottle. Beaujolais is new but once a year.

'But even not metaphorically, prostitution is more than one experience. Some kid doing twenty, thirty tricks a night in hallways and cars isn't having the same experience that someone has who performs once an evening in a good hotel.'

'I suppose someone might argue that the acts were morally the same,' Susan said.

'Ah, Suze, you're toying with me. We both know what we both think about that.'

'I know,' Susan said, 'I just like to hear how you'll put it.'

'Her morality is her business. My business is to get her free so she can take care of her business.'

'And you think setting her up with a high-priced madam in New York is the way?'

'I think it's possible. I think she has a right to be a whore if she wants to be. Just like she has the right to stop if she wants to.'

'But do you have the right to make the opportunity easy for her?'

'Yes.'

'To be a whore?'

'Yes. If she likes the work. I have no business telling her she's not supposed to like it.'

'Would you feel the same way about heroin?' Susan said.

'No. I know heroin is destructive to her. I know no such thing about the right kind of whoring.'

The fire hissed and a slow bubble of sap oozed from one end of a log. I tried less cheese and two rings of green pepper in my next sandwich.

'I think you're wrong,' Susan said. 'I think in the long run selling yourself, rather than your product, is destructive. I guess I'm willing to say that metaphorically as well as literally.'

'Maybe we're just choosing which kind of destructive exprience to offer her,' I said.

'Maybe we are,' Susan said.

CHAPTER TWENTY-NINE

Hawk wanted in.

'I want to see what this dude Poitras is like, babe,' he said.

'Always admired that streak of intellectual curiosity in you, Hawk.'

'Only go this way, one time,' Hawk said.

Susan and I sat side by side on one side of the table and Hawk sat across. We were on top of the Hyatt Regency Hotel on the

Cambridge side of the Charles. The room rotated very slowly, and you got a grandiloquent view of Boston half the time.

Susan had a large piña colada with fruit in it and was sipping it sparingly through a straw. It looked good, but I was embarrassed to order one. I had beer. Hawk had a piña colada. Nothing embarrassed him.

'It would be easier with two,' Susan said. 'And he has been in it from the start. He's got a right to be in at the finish.'

'See that,' Hawk said. 'Suze know. Except for who she hang around with she got a lot of style.'

'That's not why he wants to help bust Poitras,' I said to Susan. 'He's got as much curiosity as a parsnip. He wants to be there to remind Tony Marcus that he's in it with me.'

'Which will make Marcus more likely to keep his word,' Susan said.

'Yes.'

She reached over and patted the top of his motionless hands where they rested beside his glass. 'What a darling man you are,' Susan said, her face serious. 'Some of my best friends are black.'

Hawk burst out laughing. Several people turned their heads in mild annoyance and turned them quickly back.

'You like all honky broads,' Hawk said. 'Sentimental.'

Then they both giggled.

'When you get through with the interracial humor,' I said, 'I have a goddamned plan.'

'We listening,' Hawk said.

'Okay, when I burgled Poitras's pad . . .'

'Sexist whitey goyim,' Susan murmured, and the two of them got hysterical.

'Always talking at us minorities,' Hawk gasped. And they giggled even more. I put my chin in my hand and watched them. They were like grade-school kids who had started laughing at something innocuous and then couldn't stop. It was the only time I could recall Hawk out of control about anything. In fact, Susan was the only person I'd ever seen toward whom he showed anything but pleasant disinterest.

I tried twice again before they finally got it under control.

'When I burgled Poitras's pad, I copped a set of keys and had duplicates made,' I said. Susan was staring at me with her elbows on the table and both hands pressed against her mouth and her eyes moist.

'Um-hum,' she said. Her shoulders shook.

'Christ,' I said. 'Did George Patton have to deal with Amos and Andrea? We'll go over tonight and walk in unannounced.' I said it in a rush.

Hawk nodded.

'And we'll send April out with Susan, and Amy Gurwitz if she wants to go. Then we check that the dirty movies are still there for evidence and call the cops. Can you handle April, Suze, even if she doesn't want to go?'

She had it under control now. 'I think so. If not, Hawk can help me.'

'If he's not too busy doing his Pigmeat Markham impressions,' I said.

'I bring a stick,' he said. ''Case she get vicious.'

'Okay, let's drink up and do it,' I said.

'Just like that?' Susan said.

'If it's to be done,' I said.

'And April?' Susan said.

'You keep her in the car, and after the cops come, we'll take her back to my place and talk.' I shrugged. 'It's the best I can think of.'

'It's the best I can think of too,' Susan said.

We paid the check and went down in the elevator. Susan and I had come in her Bronco. Hawk had met us there. We decided to go in the Bronco and left Hawk's Jaguar in the parking garage.

It was dark, and the lights of Boston across the Charles made elegant starry patterns

199

against the hard early-winter blackness. We crossed the river on the B.U. bridge and Susan turned left onto Commonwealth at the NO LEFT TURN sign.

'Lawless,' I said.

'It's a dumb rule,' Susan said. 'There's no reason not to turn left there.'

'That's true,' I said.

Boston University had us surrounded as we drove down Commonwealth.

'Commanding architectural integrity,' Susan said as we passed through.

'Better-looking than some Burger Kings,' Hawk said.

In Kenmore Square the punk rockers and the college kids were feasting on pizza and subs and hot dogs and doughnuts and cheeseburgers and thick shakes and beer, and being cool. Beyond Kenmore, Commonwealth Avenue became more sedate, and after we dipped under Mass. Ave. it became positively haughty. The wide mall in the middle of Commonwealth Avenue runs flat and straight between Kenmore Square and the Public Garden. There are trees and benches in the mall and on pleasant summer days there are kids and dogs and couples, joggers, and roller skaters and Frisbee players in sufficient number to make things seem lively. Now in the dark three weeks before Christmas it was empty and cold and still.

At Fairfield, Susan turned toward the river, crossed Marlboro Street, and turned onto Beacon.

'Hydrant,' I said, and Susan saw it and pulled the Bronco into the space frontward. She began to jockey the truck back and forth trying to get parallel to the curb beside the hydrant. Hawk and I were silent as she went forward and backward, getting very little closer to the curb in the process.

'I know,' she said, 'I know I'm supposed to back in, but I hate to back in.'

Hawk and I were silent. Across the street and two doors up was Poitras's town house. There was no light on at the front door, but I could see light spilling out from around the drawn curtains.

Susan finally parked with one wheel up on the curb and the back end of the Bronco jutting aggressively out into the street.

'The hell with it,' Susan said.

Hawk and I were quiet. It had gotten very cold. There were no stars showing in the narrow channel of black sky above Beacon Street as we crossed. At the door I stopped and listened. Faintly I could hear music. I put my ear against the door. The music was a little stronger. I thought I could hear also, maybe, a faint sound of talk and movement, almost as if there were a party.

'Let's cruise around back,' I said, 'and take a peek in.'

We went in single file, no more laughing, very little talk. First me, then Susan, and Hawk a soundless, nearly invisible third.

The drapes were drawn across the French doors, but I was able to peer through a narrow gap and catch a glimpse of a crowd. The sound of music and crowd noise was louder through the glass doors. Looking up, I could see the shades drawn on all three floors with light leaking out. I gestured with my hand toward the street and we walked back down the alley to Fairfield and around the corner back onto Beacon.

'It's a large party,' I said.

'Friday night,' Hawk said.

'Never set up a raid on a Friday night,' I said.

'Can we do it anyway?' Susan said.

Hawk looked at me.

I said, 'Why not. I got a key. Let's go in and have a look. If the party's big and wild enough, no one will pay any attention.'

Hawk nodded once. Susan said, 'Party,

party.' In the dim light from the streetlamp I could see her eyes wide and the slight indentation around her mouth that meant repressed excitement.

We went to the door and I knocked lightly. No answer. I tried the knob. It was locked. I took out the duplicate keys and opened the front door. The place must have been soundproofed because when the door was open the blast of sound was overpowering. Hard rock music thumped and voices were shrill and glasses clattered. We stepped inside and closed the door. The air was thick with tobacco smoke and pot and the smell of booze, and hot with human scent. We took off our coats in the hallway and laid them across the umbrella stand. While we were doing that a big surly-looking man appeared at the end of the hall and walked toward us. He was wearing a blue blazer that was too small for him and the gun he wore under it made a clear bulge. He had long muttonchop sideburns and his hair was longish, so that it trailed over his collar in back. Hawk smiled.

'What are you people doing here?' the surly man said.

Hawk smiled some more. 'We been over there,' he said vaguely, pointing with his right hand across his body at the wall next to his shoulder. The surly man was close now and frowning as he looked in the direction that Hawk was pointing.

He said, 'Huh?'

And Hawk hit him with the edge of his pointing right hand across the bridge of his nose. I could hear the bone break. The man grunted, put his hands toward his face, and Hawk hit him, still with the edge of his right hand, this time just back of the left ear. The surly man's hands never made it to his face. They dropped straight in front of him and the surly man's body followed. He fell face forward on the floor and he lay still. I opened the front door. Hawk and I each took hold of the back of his coat collar and dragged him outside. Hawk reached down and slipped his gun out of its holster and we shoved him over the ornamental railing in behind the bare winter shrubs. Then we came back in and Susan closed the door behind us. Her eyes were shiny. Hawk handed her the surly man's gun, a short-barreled Colt detective special. 'Stick that in your purse,' he said. 'Don't want to leave it laying around.' Susan plonked it into her shoulder bag. It disappeared easily. She could have kept a collection of blunderbusses in there without being discovered.

We followed the noise and smoke and smell along the hall and down the three steps to the living room. Susan's hand was on my arm.

Susan said, 'Jesus Christ.'

The room was a swarm of debauchery, a maelstrom of naked and part-naked limbs and torsos. It looked like a feverish animation of one of those Gustave Doré illustrations for *The Inferno*. Somewhere in the swarm rock music was playing at top volume on a good stereo. The smoke hung under the ceiling, eddying around the table lamps as the hot light bulbs caused a tiny thermal updraft. The thump of the music made a discernible vibration in the stairs as we stood looking in. I let Hawk stand in front of us in case Poitras or Amy or April spotted us.

The laughter that had filtered out through the French doors as I stood there in the dark a few moments ago now snarled with the music, raw and harsh and gilded at the edges with hysteria. Slicing through the thick smell of pot and booze and perfume and sweat was a thin medicinal smell I wasn't sure of. Ether maybe. The heat was threatening. The air seemed hard to breathe. Hawk was whistling softly through his teeth again. He was less than a foot away and I could barely make out the tune; it was 'Stars and Stripes Forever.'

'Thank God it's Friday,' I murmured to Susan.

The room was the same one in which I'd had my correct beer with Amy the first time I'd come, but just barely. Much of the furniture was gone and what remained had been pushed against the walls. On the bar there were half-gallon bottles of vodka and saucers of bright capsules. I could see reds and yellows and blues from where I was. There were plastic glasses in a stack and a large bag of ice tipped over and partially melted in a big puddle near the vodka. There was jug wine and some bourbon and a freezer-size baggy of grass open and some spilling. The lights around the edges of the room were bright and, reflecting off the beige walls, lit the living room like a movie set. On the wall to the right of the bar a large-screen TV was showing in color a video-tape in which two naked women and one naked man in a shower stall were involved in active foreplay while the shower head fanned a steady spray of water down on them. The actors appeared to be speaking lines, but they were soundless in the face of the music and the laughter.

'We better move down among them,' I said

to Susan and Hawk. 'We're too out of place up here looking down.' They nodded and, Hawk first, we went down the three steps and into the maw of the beast. T. J. Eckleberg, where are you when I need you?

I said, 'Pay attention to those movies, Suze. Pick up your technique a little.'

'Anything anyone in this room or on that screen is doing,' Susan said quietly, 'I never wish to do with you ever.'

'Oh,' I said. 'Close your eyes, then, and hang on to me.'

The men in the room were generally middle-aged, the women generally children. Most of the people were sprawled on the floor, and while there seemed to be a good deal of fondling going on, I saw no actual intercourse. Nothing déclassé here. We skirted a couple on the floor near the big-screen television. He had short gray hair and a clipped gray mustache and a white broadcloth shirt and a red bow tie. She was wearing only a camisole. He had one hand under the camisole as she giggled and tipped a glass of what appeared to be straight vodka against his lower lip for him to drink. Her fingernails were painted blue and so were her toenails. She appeared to be maybe fifteen. A tall angular man with gold-rimmed glasses was trying to dance to the shattering music. His partner was a tall still-faced blond girl with a long single braid down her back. She wore high-heeled shoes and tight designer jeans and no shirt. The strap of her black bra made a thin line across her white back. They were having trouble dancing because they were both drunk and because the man was trying to waltz to the music, holding the girl close against him. He bumped into me as we circled the room and said, ''Scush me,' and stumbled away. As we moved on he tried to dip with his partner and they fell down, she on top of him. They stayed there.

Susan said in my ear, 'That's Foster Carmichael. He's an associate commissioner of education.'

'What dedication,' I said. 'Devotes even his weekends to kids.'

A black-haired kid with a freckled Irish face was standing on the coffee table against the far wall doing a slow strip-tease to music that must have come from a different drummer. She moved slowly, her face fixed in adolescent imitation of a sultry smile as she struggled with her clothes. She was too zonked to figure it out, but it was hard to strip in real clothes. It was hard to scrunch out of your designer jeans and look like

208

Gypsy Rose Lee at the same time.

We didn't see April in the room, or Amy, or Poitras. Susan saw two other people she recognized, and I spotted a state rep that I knew. As we wedged back toward the stairs a man on the floor ran his hand up Susan's calf. I stepped on his stomach and he took his hand away.

'A real compliment,' I said in her ear. 'Thinks you're a high school kid.'

'And he thinks you're a bully,' she said.

'He's correct.'

We made it back to the stairs. The sweat was soaking through my shirt, my collar felt as limp as an old dandelion. I realized I was holding Susan's hand. Hawk's face was shiny with sweat as he joined us on the steps.

'Sure do know how to have a good time, don't they?' Hawk said.

The man whose stomach I had stepped on was throwing up on the floor. Nobody paid him any attention.

'Trendy,' I said.

The hall that had seemed oppressive when we came in now seemed cool and open after the living room. I led the way upstairs, still holding Susan's hand, with Hawk behind her. When we got to the second floor there were three December–May couples in the hallway, sitting on the floor in a circle passing a bong around. They paid no attention to us as we went past them and looked into the master bedroom. In the bed was a man and three young girls. All were without clothes. They were busy. None of the girls was April so I closed the door. There were people busy in Poitras's office also, using his swivel chair—which was tricky.

'In a swivel chair?' Susan said.

'To seek, to strive, and not to yield,' I said.

There was more activity in the guest room, and even something energetic happening in the bathroom. None of it involved Poitras or the two girls. They were on the third floor.

CHAPTER THIRTY

When we opened the door to the photo shop, Poitras was sitting in a canvas-backed director's chair, spilling out on both sides of it. Amy stood on one side of him holding a tray of canapés from which Poitras was eating as we entered. April stood behind him, her hands on his shoulders, massaging the base of his neck quietly. Sitting opposite was a middle-sized fiftyish man with a round face and an unhealthy-looking flush to his skin. He was wearing a gray pinstriped double-breasted suit and a conservative soft hat with a narrow brim. He looked like an unsuccessful diplomat. Behind the diplomat, leaning against the wall looking bored, with his arms folded, was an overweight slugger wearing a suede trench coat. The diplomat was reading a large sheet of lined paper. A half-drunk glass of something with a lime wedge in it was on the floor beside him. When we walked in they all turned and looked at us. Not startled, just annoyed. I looked at Hawk and then toward the slugger. Hawk nodded.

Poitras said, 'I'm sorry, this is private up here . . .' and then recognized me and Susan.

I said, 'Say, Mitchell, you know how to throw some swell party.'

Without looking up from his lined paper the diplomat said, 'Didn't Mickey tell you the third floor was off limits? Get the fuck out of here.'

The overweight slugger was still leaning against the wall, but he had uncrossed his arms and he didn't look bored.

I said, 'We had a communications problem with Mickey when we arrived and had to ask him to leave.'

The diplomat looked up. Poitras said, 'He's a private cop, Hal.'

The diplomat said, 'What the fuck are you running here, you fat jerk? A private cop? Who's that with him, the fucking police commissioner?'

'I don't know, Hal. I don't know what he's doing here. He's been bothering me about the girls.'

'You fucking baby raper, I shoulda known better than to try to do business with a goddamn child molester.' He looked at the slugger. 'Get them outta here, Vince.'

The slugger straightened from the wall and Hawk pointed a handgun at him. 'I think Vince overmatched,' Hawk said in his friendly, gliding voice. He grinned at the diplomat. 'You too, Hal.' I went and took the slugger's gun and dropped it in my jacket pocket.

Everyone was still looking at the gun, steady in Hawk's hand, pointing at Vince. I went to the files and opened the top drawer. It was still full of evidence. I stepped across to Hal and took his sheet of lined paper from his hands. It was an inventory list for video cassettes with titles like *Grade School Gals* and *Teeny Boppers*. I folded it twice and put it in my shirt pocket. I didn't bother to pat Hal

212

down. Guys like him never carried guns. They had employees like Vince to do that.

'Okay, April,' I said. 'You go with Mrs. Silverman.'

'No.'

'Yeah. Go sit in the car with her until we get through in here and then we'll go back to my place and have some milk and Fig Newtons, and we'll talk.'

'No.'

'You too, Amy, you should go too.'

She didn't even look up. She had her head down, looking at the plate of canapés, and she shook it.

'In a little while there's going to be cops here,' I said.

'Cops?' Hal said.

'Yeah. Soon as the girls are out I'm going to call them.'

Hal said, 'That's no way to make a buck.'

'Neither is this,' I said.

Hal looked at Hawk. 'Hey, man,' he said. 'Be smart. There's some bread to be made here.'

Hawk grinned. Without taking his eyes off Vince he said to me, 'Hear that "Hey, man"? This a soul brother—see how he know how to talk to us darkies? He say "Hey, man" and he say "bread."' Hawk stretched the *bread* out in a burlesque jive accent.

The diplomat raised his hands. 'Hey, no offense. Black, white, makes no difference to me. There's a lot of money involved here. I'm talking about giving you guys a piece of it.'

Poitras was motionless in all this. Amy had put her canapés aside and taken his left hand. She held it in her lap with both of hers.

I said, 'April. You don't have a choice. Go with Susan or we'll take you. Amy, you can go or stay.'

Still without looking up, Amy said in a voice as small as her prospects, 'Stay.' There was something almost touching about the ugly fat man sitting there in his Thom McAn shoes with a little kid holding his hand and refusing to leave. Love? A turkey like that? Someone loved him? I shook my head.

'Go ahead, April,' I said. I was beginning to feel tight inside. I'd been in here too long with the bizarre sexuality and the affectless children and the ugly men. There was force in my voice. April nodded.

She said, 'Bye, Amy,' and walked out the door. Susan went with her.

I said to Poitras, 'There is a gentleman of some influence whose name we won't mention. He has offices in the South End and you served him as a supplier of youthful

214

whores.'

Poitras said, 'I don't know what you're talking about.' But there was no bite in his growl now. He was scared.

'Yeah you do. This gentleman has asked me to remind you that no mention be made of his name or his relationship to you. He says that some really dire things will happen to you if he gets involved.'

Hawk glanced at me out of the corner of his eye. 'Dire?' he said.

'I was dean's list once in school,' I said.

'I can tell.'

I said to Poitras, 'You understand what I told you?'

He nodded.

'I got a deal with this gentleman,' I said. 'So I want to be sure.'

'I won't say nothing. I know what'd happen,' Poitras said. I could barely hear him. His growl had become a mumble. Amy clutched his hand in both hers, rubbing it with the thumb of her top hand.

I looked around the lab. No phone. There was one in the office below. 'Last chance, Amy. I'm going to call the fuzz.'

She shook her head. I said to Hawk, 'Think you'll be safe here without me?'

'I can always scream,' he said.

Through the door to the lab I heard some commotion sounds from downstairs; then I heard Susan's voice.

She yelled, 'Spenser,' and there was a sound in her yell I'd not heard from her before. She was scared. I headed across the room. Hawk looked at me and then at Poitras and his group.

'Fuck them,' he said. 'Where they going to go?'

As I pounded down the stairs he was right behind me. There was no one on the second floor. And as I rounded the landing and headed toward the first I saw Susan in the middle of a crowd of men and girls.

April was separated from her by a man wearing dark glasses. His shirt was open nearly to the waist and there was a bright smear of lipstick across the right side of his mouth.

'She's trying to kidnap me,' April was yelling. 'She's trying to take me away. Help me.'

Susan is never graceless and rarely stupid. She made no attempt to argue. Instead she pushed the man in front of her and took hold of April. The man with the shades objected.

'Who you shoving, baby?' he said, and grabbed Susan by the upper arms.

216

I was three steps from the bottom when he gasped with pain and doubled forward. His hands slid from Susan's arms.

April yelled, 'Help me, please help me.'

The crowd closed around Susan and I hit the bottom stair and started to throw bodies out of the way. Someone punched me on the side of the face and I flailed out with an elbow and shoved somebody else's face and I was beside Susan. Somebody tried to bite my upper arm. I lunged my shoulder into them and they stopped.

'Never mind April,' I said to Susan. 'get out of here and call McNeely in vice.'

A young woman climbed on my back with her hands scratching at my face. I reached up and pulled her face forward with my left hand and when it was in sight I punched it with my right. Across the hall I saw Hawk pick someone up and ram him backward through the stair railing. The uprights splintered and the railing cracked in two. I jammed my way backward toward the front door, keeping Susan beside me. A fist hit my stomach, another hit me above the eye, and I could feel blood begin to flow. I kicked a groin. I smacked a gray mustache. There was a mass of bodies behind me. I spun. I whacked someone with my forearm, banged two heads together, and wedged me and Susan through the gap that formed when the two people fell. We were against the front door. I put my foot against someone's stomach and shoved, buttressing my back against the door. For a moment there was room. I opened the door and shoved Susan out. The door slammed shut behind her from the weight of thrashing people. Some were fighting. Some were trying to get away. Everyone was drunk and stoned and both and crazy with sex and dope and booze and music and heat and crowd. Vince, Hal's slugger, came charging down the stairs with Hal behind him. He tried to hit Hawk with a brass candlestick and missed, and Hawk hit him three times, his hands a mere blur in the maelstrom, and the slugger went down out of sight in the turmoil of men and girls. Someone tried to choke me. I brought my hands up together to break the grip and then chopped to the side of a neck, where it joined a shoulder. I stepped on someone that tried to bite my ankle, I punched someone in front of me. I half turned and drove my elbow into someone behind me. There was no gender anymore. I made no attempt to figure out if I was hitting men or girls. No sexist I. Someone half got me in the groin and I could feel that sick feeling that only men know, but it was a glancing blow and the feeling didn't get bad. Someone spit on me. Someone hit my shoulder with a hard object. I kneed a crotch and banged a nose. We had roiled through the hall and into the sunken living room, going down the three steps as if riding a wave. A small man with a goatee was picked up and thrown against the wall and I was beside Hawk. He moved as if he were dancing, with a kind of joyful and vicious rhythm. The sweat rolled down his face. His bald head gleamed. There was a cut on his cheek and blood mixed pinkish with the sweat. His arms swelled and relaxed inside the sleeves of his gray flannel jacket. As I jostled against him I could hear him still whistling through his teeth his soft private whistle: 'Stars and Stripes Forever.' A goddamned patriot. Somebody got a good shot into my jaw and my chimes rang for a minute. I hit back, and hit somebody else, and kicked at a kneecap. At my angle I could look into the hall, and as I put my open hand on someone's yelling face and shoved, I saw Poitras and Amy standing on the stairs halfway down from the second floor, holding hands, looking in, uncertain and scared. I caught a wild roundhouse punch on my forearm and demonstrated a much better way on someone's chin. An ear flashed across my line of vision—I hammered it with the side of my left fist. Don't want to break your hand on a head. I felt slippery with sweat and a little drunk with the fumes and the contact and the way my blood pounded in my head. When I'd seen Susan in the mob there had been an adrenaline spurt enough to launch a space probe. It was carrying me now. Someone jumped at me and I caught it crotch and shirtfront and helped it on past me over my left shoulder. It smashed into two other people and all three went down. Other people stepped on them. Hawk hit two faces simultaneously, one with each hand and I realized he was punching unconsciously in time to his whistle. In a fight things slow down when you are really pumped up, and it all seems like a Sam Peckinpah movie with bodies floating around and blood flowing slowly. I felt loose and warmed up and full of oxygen. I had another cut now, I could taste the blood in my mouth. Not the nose, I thought. The nose had been broken maybe eight times. Maybe this time it would be something else. Somebody waded in toward us with a fireplace poker. He caught Hawk on the shoulder and I grabbed the end and yanked it away from him as Hawk hit him with the dark blur of his quick hands. Hawk had the fastest hands I'd ever seen. He could catch flies even in the summer when they were frisky. A wineglass broke against the wall behind me and I hit an open mouth with two excellent left hooks. I could catch summer flies too, now that I thought of it. The press of the crowd was thinning. I was getting room to maneuver, to pull back and punch full out. Hawk and I had made progress. I drove my heel into an instep and my elbow into a throat. I took a step forward and landed a textbook overhand right and was rocked from behind by someone who hit me on the side of the head with something more than a fist. I turned, ducking as I turned, and saw a furled umbrella upraised and punched in under it and heard a groan and saw it skitter away on the floor as I turned back and caught someone's lunge with my open hands at chest level. I shoved him away and he stumbled back and smashed through the French doors. Cold air rushed in and I filled my lungs as I knocked someone's punch off with my right forearm and landed my left on a nose. The nose spurted blood. *Better yours than mine.*

And then it was over. Hawk and I stood in

a small open space with people stumbling, or fallen, gasping for breath and bleeding, in a circle around us. Men and girls with clothing torn, blood-spattered, and sweaty with an occasional splotch of vomit or spit spoiling a shirt, and the cold, clean air streaming in the broken French doors starting to dry the sweat that had even soaked through my jacket. I looked at Hawk. His jacket too was black with sweat across the back.

Hawk looked at me and grinned. 'You right, Mitchell sure do know how to throw a party.'

'Lucky he doesn't have any strong friends,' I said. 'I might have got my nose broken.'

'Who could tell?' Hawk said.

There was a loud pounding at the front door and at the same time four cops pushed through the broken French doors and pointed guns at everyone. McNeely had arrived.

CHAPTER THIRTY-ONE

The genie we'd let out of the bottle was a lot bigger than any of us were going to know for a long time. But sitting in Poitras's living room drinking Schlitz beer from a long-necked bottle, I knew my nose was whole. Hawk and I had washed up. And one of the prowl car cops had brought in a first-aid kit and patched us up. The cut inside my mouth would need a couple of stitches. There were a lot of bruises that would swell and discolor. But my nose was hale and intact. I stroked it with pleasure. The prowlie was putting a butterfly closure on a cut in Hawk's eyebrow.

'How's his nose?' I said.

'Fine,' he said.

'Oh.'

The cop looked over at me.

'You sound disappointed,' he said.

Hawk said, 'He five breaks ahead of me. He hoping I'd catch up.'

Four plainclothes vice squad cops were busy hauling out incriminating evidence in cardboard cartons. Poitras was in the kitchen with McNeely and an assistant DA. They were explaining his rights to him. Amy refused to leave him and they had only brought one policewoman, and she was busy, and they didn't know what to do with her. So as they talked in the kitchen she sat beside him in a straight chair and patted his thigh.

The diplomat had vanished and so had the surly-looking man named Mickey that Hawk and I had thrown over the railing when we came in. But Vince was still around. He was just coming around now and he wasn't talking because his jaw was broken. April was gone. The other guests were in ragged clusters trying to get their attire straightened out—the vomit washed off, the blood wiped away. Trying to get their eyes focused and their brains reintegrated. There were three reporters and a news photographer there and the guests were avoiding them and covering their faces.

The policewoman said to the photographer, 'Most of these girls are juveniles.'

The photographer nodded and concentrated on the men. His strobe made small lightning flashes in the room. The assistant commissioner of education kept a handkerchief over his face and murmured to the vice cop who was taking his name that he was a friend of a city councilman. The cop nodded and asked to see his driver's license. The state rep kept asking to speak with McNeely and being told to sit down. 'Lieutenant will get to you when he gets to you.'

The state rep told the reporter that he'd be in touch with his editor and the reporter said,

'Whyn't you get in touch with yourself.' And the photographer snapped his picture.

McNeely came out of the kitchen and gestured one of the detectives in to watch Poitras. Or maybe to watch the assistant DA.

'You know the girl?' he said to me.

'Yes. Name's Amy Gurwitz.'

'You know where she lives?'

'Here.'

'She told me that. But hasn't she got parents or something?'

'Ask her,' I said.

'I did ask her. What the fuck do you think I'm asking you for?'

I shrugged. Beyond him I could see her in the kitchen in her straight chair. She was still patting Poitras's knee. He had his head hanging forward and his shoulders slumped, slouched in the chair so that he was almost shapeless, his stomach covering most of his thighs as he sat. There was nothing left. He was shapeless with defeat.

'Love is a many-splendored thing, McNeely,' I said. 'She wants to stay with him.'

'Don't lecture me about love, cowboy,' McNeely said. 'I got six kids. Where he's going she can't go.'

'How about you haul her down to Charles

Street?' I said.

'You know we don't put women in Charles Street,' McNeely said. 'Besides, she's a kid. Besides, she hasn't done anything that I know of. We got nothing to arrest her for.'

'She says she lives here?' I said.

'Yeah.'

'Why don't you leave her here?'

McNeely spread his hands and looked around at the room with a look that encompassed the whole building. 'She's sixteen years old,' he said.

'You got a better idea?'

He looked around again. At the litter of bottles and cigarettes, pills, snack food ground into the carpet, people grouped in frightened huddles waiting for the trip to night court. He breathed the smell of booze and dope and sweat and vomit.

'No,' he said. 'Maybe later I can get somebody to send a social worker over.'

'I'll look in on her occasionally,' I said. 'And my friend Susan will too.'

Hawk had rummaged behind the bar and came out with two more bottles of Schlitz.

'Man got a fine taste in long necks,' Hawk said. He handed me one. 'Sorry 'bout you being on duty, Lieutenant.'

McNeely ignored him. I took a long pull

on the beer bottle. It felt clean and cold going down. I could use clean and cold for a while.

I said, 'The night is young, McNeely. Hawk and me got places to go, people to see. You need us anymore?'

He shook his head. He was staring into the kitchen. 'Not now,' he said. 'Somebody in the DA's office will want to talk with you one of these days. We'll let you know.'

Hawk and I walked out into the cold night. There were police cars all over the street, their blue lights turning, the mechanical sound of radios rasping and crackling in some of them. A station wagon with the tailgate down was half full of cardboard boxes. A motorcycle cop in a helmet and leather jacket was directing traffic past the congestion and a bunch of Beacon Street neighbors were standing around hugging themselves and staring. To the right down across the street near the corner of Fairfield, Susan's big red-and-white Bronco stuck out into the traffic. People gave way as we walked towards it, looking at both of us, noticing the Band-Aids and the bruises, not saying anything.

'Could of saved a lot of energy if we'd burned a couple people in there early. Nothing like a couple gunshots to clear an area,' Hawk said.

'Too crowded,' I said. 'No way to know who you're shooting. Most people in there didn't deserve to get shot.'

Hawk grinned. 'Deserve,' he said. He spat some pinkish saliva onto the sidewalk under the streetlight.

When we got to the car, April was sitting in the front seat with Susan.

CHAPTER THIRTY-TWO

'She came with me on her own,' Susan said. Hawk and I had climbed into the back past April's tipped-forward seat.

'I called the police and then I came back and stood outside. Several people came out, including the man from upstairs, and then April came out and saw me and walked over. When the police came we walked back to the car to get warm.'

Susan drove slowly past the Poitras house, waved on by the motorcycle cop.

'Why do you suppose they wear those high boots?' Susan said. 'Is there some motorcycle reason for it?'

'Makes them think they cavalry,' Hawk said.

Susan turned up Gloucester and then left onto Marlboro. 'I assume we're going to your place,' she said.

'Yeah. You need a ride to your car, Hawk?'

He shook his head. 'I'll walk down from your place and catch a cab in front of the Ritz.'

Susan pulled up half a block from my front door. 'My God,' she said, 'there's a parking spot.'

Hawk and I were silent.

'I can't stand it again,' Susan said. She opened the door and got out. April got out as soon as Susan did. Hawk got out and stood with them while I backed the Bronco into the first space I'd seen open on Marlboro Street since Labor Day weekend. Then I got out and joined them.

'Send me a bill,' I said to Hawk.

He nodded, nodded at April, kissed Susan good-bye, and headed down Marlboro, walking as he did everything, without seeming effort, moving to the rhythm of some internal and volitionless mechanism. I watched him go for a minute and then turned and gestured toward the apartment.

'In case you have to wee wee,' I said to April. 'There's a place upstairs.'

'I don't need to,' she said.

We went up. My apartment smelled empty. It was neat, the cleaning person had been there. Somehow that made it worse. It looked like one of those display rooms in department stores.

'Anyone hungry?' I said.

April shrugged. Susan said, 'Yes.'

'I'll make something while we talk,' I said. 'A drink while I'm cooking?'

Susan had coffee. April wanted Pepsi, but settled for a beer. Me too.

April sat beside Susan at the counter. On the other side of the counter I was working my magic. While I worked it, I talked to April.

'You got a plan, kid?'

'For what?'

'For what you're going to do tomorrow?'

'Can I stay here tonight?'

'Yes.'

April drank a little beer from her glass. I could see she didn't like it much. Hard to warm up to someone who didn't like beer. Suze had managed to overcome that handicap, but it wasn't a good start.

'And tomorrow?' I said.

She shrugged. 'You gonna drag me out to see Mommy and Poppy?'

'No.'

April looked at Susan. Susan smiled neutrally and drank some coffee. She could smile a hole through Mount McKinley whenever she felt like it, and I was never able to figure out how she could modify the smile to neutral, or even, when she chose, disapproval.

I had a country pâté I'd made from lamb and duck and pistachio nuts and an anchovy. I sliced that up and made sandwiches on whole wheat bread. I put the platter of sandwiches out with a dish of bread-and-butter pickles that Susan and I had made in September from a bunch of small funny-looking cucumbers we'd bought at a farm stand in Danvers.

'Well, what are you gonna do with me?' April said.

'What do you want me to do?' I said.

Susan picked up half a sandwich and ate a bite. 'Do you have any of that peach chutney that Paul gave you?' Susan said. I did. I got the jar out and put it on the counter. Susan took a small forkful and put it on her saucer. She took a dab from the plate and ate it and took another bite of the sandwich.

April looked at her sandwich. 'What is this,' she said.

'Pâté,' I said.

'What's that?'

'It's like meatloaf,' I said.

Susan ate a little more chutney.

'You got any white bread?' April said.

Susan's eyes gleamed at me over her coffee cup.

'No.'

'What's that jam?' April said.

'Chutney,' I said. 'It's sort of a fruit pickle, it's not jam.'

April took a very small bite of the pâté sandwich and showed no more pleasure than she had with the beer.

'Sorry,' I said. 'I'm out of Wonder Bread and bologna. Would you like peanut butter? Or toast and jam?'

'Toast,' she said.

I sliced bread and put it in the toaster. I put out some Trappist boysenberry jam. I knew she'd prefer grape jelly, but I was out of that too.

'So what are you going to do tomorrow?' I said to April while her toast was toasting.

She shrugged again.

'You want to go home?'

'No.'

'You want to go back to Providence?'

She shook her head.

'Want a job?'

'Doing what?' she said.

'What would you say your most marketable skill was?' I said.

She made a small unfunny laugh. 'Fucking,' she said and glanced sideways at Susan, checking the effect. Susan ate a pickle, holding it in the very tip of her thumb and forefinger and taking a bite out of it. She never ate anything in one bite.

'I think I won't ask your second most marketable skill,' I said.

'Wise,' Susan said. 'April, let's see if we can cut through a little of the cynical disaffection. Spenser and I both think you're too young to be alone and directionless. We are trying to get you to help us think of something for you to do. I am less sentimental than he is. I might take you back to your parents' home, leave you there, and let them deal with the problem. But he won't do that. He would see that as merely postponing the problem, or giving it to someone else. On the assumption that you'll run away again.'

'I didn't go to all this trouble,' I said, 'to have you back with Red turning tricks in the Zone.'

'Maybe I like that,' she said.

'You don't,' I said. 'I saw the picture of

your house on the wall in that crib you were living in on Chandler Street.'

'So what does that mean?'

'I carried a picture of my house through nearly two years in Korea,' I said. 'I know why you had it on your wall, and I know what it means.'

Her toast had popped and I buttered it and put it out with a jar of jam and a spoon. She ate some.

'So what do you think I should do?' April said. 'I'd rather be a whore than live at home.'

I looked at Susan. She widened her eyes and shook her head—one of her don't-ask-me motions.

'How about you move in with Amy?'

'I don't like her,' April said. 'She's feebie. And her old man's going to jail. She won't have any money.'

'So we're back to whore again,' I said.

She nodded. I ate some of my sandwich and drank some of my beer.

'How do you like whoring?' I said.

'It's okay sometimes. Sometimes the guys are nice. It's not bad.'

'What's the worst thing about it?' Susan said.

'Creepy guys, being alone with them in the

234

back of a car or in some toilet or a dump like you saw.'

'How many tricks a night with Red?' I said.

'Ten, fifteen.'

I got up and got more beer and sat back down on my side of the counter and looked at her. 'If you're going to be a whore, why be a cheap one?'

She shrugged. Made me think of Paul Giacomin when I'd first met him. That was two years ago. Now he was different. He hadn't even come for Thanksgiving. He'd stayed with his girl friend. He didn't shrug like that anymore. At least not at me.

'If you'll go with me,' I said, 'tomorrow I'm going to take you down to New York and introduce you to a woman named Patricia Utley, who runs a high-priced and selective prostitution business.'

I heard Susan let her breath out softly.

'You want me to be a whore?' April said.

'No,' I said, 'but I know at least one good woman who used to be a whore for Patricia Utley. If you're going to be a whore, at least we can upgrade your level of whoring. You'd do one trick a night and not every night. You'd be dealing with a relatively civilized clientele. You'd learn how to dress and talk and order wine in a restaurant. You'd be better off than you are now.'

'In New York?'

'Yes.'

'I never been to New York.'

'I'll take you,' I said. 'And if she likes you and you like her and she's willing to take you on, she'll look out for you.'

'You're really going to introduce me to a madam?'

'Best I can think of,' I said. 'You decide you don't like it, let me know and I'll come down and get you and bring you back.'

'Is it in a nice part of New York?'

I nodded. The sandwiches were gone. I was on my third beer. Susan was sitting very quietly now, watching and listening and not saying a word.

'Should I?' April said to Susan.

'No,' Susan said. 'I don't think you should. I think you should go home, and I will try, with you, to get you and your parents into counseling. I cannot believe that being a whore is a better choice.'

April looked back at me.

'I won't urge you,' I said. 'Susan may be right. You have to decide. You have to judge whether your parents would seek counseling, whether you would, and if it would help.'

'And,' Susan said, 'you have to judge how you really feel about being a prostitute.'

'If you want me to be a whore, why'd you take me away from Red and them in the first place?' April said. Nobody says a whore has to be smart.

I took a deep breath. 'I don't want you to be a whore or not a whore. I want you to be free. I want you to choose what you do and I want you to live a better life than you were living in the sheep ranch in Providence. If your choice is between growing up with Red and growing up with Patricia Utley, I think you're better off with Utley.'

We were all quiet then, Susan and I looking at April, April with her plump, sullen little face clenched in confusion staring at the counter. I got up and cleared away the dishes. Susan made herself another cup of coffee.

'Would you come with me?' April said to Susan.

'To see Patricia Utley?'

'Yes. You and him both?'

Susan was quiet for a moment.

I said, 'She can't, April. What happens to a guidance counselor who places students in a whorehouse?'

'You think it's okay,' April said to me.

237

'I do, or I might,' I said, 'But I'm not on the school committee in Smithfield. People rarely get elected to school committees because they have a broad and flexible sense of life's possibilities.'

April said, 'Huh?'

Susan said, 'I'll go with you, April.'

'If I don't like it I don't have to stay, do I?' April said.

'No,' I said.

'Okay. I'll talk to this lady,' April said.

CHAPTER THIRTY-THREE

It was about two thirty in the morning. April was asleep on my couch. I was showered and aspirined and retaped and lying in bed beside Susan.

'Is this crazy?' I said.

She turned her head on the pillow and looked at me and said, 'I think so.'

'You think it will work out if she goes home and you try to arrange therapy?'

Her eyes were lovely, dark and deep. 'No,' Susan said. 'I don't think it would.'

'So the best we can do is give her a chance to sell her body less often for more money,' I

said.

Susan was quiet.

'I know how much you care about your job and your profession,' I said to her. 'The kid doesn't understand, but I know what it took for you to say you'd go visit the madam with her.'

'I can't put the profession ahead of the people it's supposed to serve,' Susan said. 'It would be like teachers who care more about education than students.'

'Because it's right doesn't make it easy,' I said. 'I admire you quite a lot.'

Susan's eyes were much closer. 'You made me what I am today, big boy.'

'And I did a hell of a job,' I murmured.

Susan rested her head against my chest. I turned the light out with my free hand.

'You think she'll stay with Utley?' Susan murmured.

'Yes,' I said.

'You think her parents would really care if they found out?'

'They shouldn't find out,' I said. 'They'd think they were supposed to care, but in fact, I think, they'd be relieved. We'll work up a story for them.'

'You think the Child Study Department would give me extra credit for field work on this one?' Susan said, her voice had that fading liquid quality it got as she was falling asleep.

'I think they would get a sack full of rocks and form a circle about you,' I said.

'They might be justified.'

'Yeah, but who'd throw the first stone?'

Susan made a snuggling motion with her face and pressed her nose against my chest. I closed my eyes. I could feel the heavy darkness settle.

'Spenser?' Susan's voice was remote now.

'Yeah?'

'Do you think we're doing the right thing?'

'If I knew that,' I said, and my own voice was far away, 'I could throw the first stone.'

The publishers hope that this Large Print Book has brought you pleasurable reading. Each title is designed to make the text as easy to see as possible. G. K. Hall Large Print Books are available from your library and your local bookstore. Or you can receive information on upcoming and current Large Print Books by mail and order directly from the publisher. Just send your name and address to:

G. K. Hall & Co.
70 Lincoln Street
Boston, Mass. 02111

or call, toll-free:

1–800–343–2806